EX TEMPORE

EX
TEMPORE

Tiina Utoslahti

The Book Guild Ltd

First published in Great Britain in 2022 by
The Book Guild Ltd
The Book Guild
Unit E2, Airfield Business Park
Harrison Road
Market Harborough
Leicestershire, LE16 7UL
Freephone: 0800 999 2982
www.bookguild.co.uk
Email: info@bookguild.co.uk
Twitter: @bookguild

Typeset in 11pt Adobe Garamond Pro

Printed and bound in Great Britain by 4edge Limited

ISBN 978 1914471 056

British Library Cataloguing in Publication Data.
A catalogue record for this book is available from the British Library.

To my husband Kari

ONE

"THIS CANNOT BE REAL!"

Pharmacist Sanna Blinck stood in the threshold of Oulu's Third Pharmacy spirits storeroom, frozen on the spot. She had intended to get a few small bottles of sanitiser to take up to the counter, but the unexpected sight just inside the door made her reconsider it. There was a young man lying on the floor, reminding her of natural-size dummies they used on their skills tests during her nurse education. A dim lamp high on the ceiling emphasised the impression of the colour on his face. Sanna stood frozen, for a time that seemed to last an eternity, before she breathed her first thought aloud.

Her tension was released when Kristiina, peeking from the coffee room doorway, asked an inquisitive question: "What the heck are you doing at the door?" She had turned to look at Sanna's stiff position and her pale face.

Sanna turned her head in Kristiina's direction. "A strange guy is lying on the floor in here. Or I am just seeing things."

Kristiina took a few running steps in order to get to Sanna's side. She looked inside the storeroom. "That's Mikael!"

Her eyes were like saucers when she looked at Sanna.

"Hold that door while I take a look what's wrong with him."

Kristiina moved so she could hold the heavy fire door, stopping the door pump from making the door slam shut, while Sanna examined unconscious Mikael. Sanna kneeled on the top of the metallic threshold and leaned forwards. Sanna turned to Kristiina, standing at the door: "Do you have a torch down here?"

"Yes, it's somewhere here, just a second."

Kristiina fetched the torch and passed it to Sanna. She pointed it straight to Mikael's face. His open eyes were like black holes in his lurid, pale face. When the light fixed on the bloody goo on the right side of his head, Sanna flinched backwards and fell on the cellar floor. The blow emptied her lungs so she could only croak: "Call the police here, now!"

Kristiina stared back at her: "We have to go back up; there is no signal down here."

Sanna crawled up from the floor. They closed the storeroom door with shaking hands and climbed up the stairs slowly together. Sanna was grateful for Kristiina's company.

Once upstairs, they headed straight to the apothecary's office, paying no attention to inquisitive glances from their workmates. There, they spoke almost in unison, repeating their story thrice before Martti realised that they were telling the truth. After a phone call, they all returned downstairs. When opening the storage room door, Sanna's thoughts were wandering. Part of her hoped that Mikael's body was only a hallucination. She saw from Kristiina's gaze that she shared her wish. However, Mikael's body still lay there.

For a moment, Martti stood in the doorway; his face was frozen. He seemed to age years in a few moments.

They returned upstairs. Martti walked straight into a space between checking table and the counter to cast an eye on the small waiting area. Two elderly ladies sat on the chairs set in the waiting area, with a small table between them, covered with a few magazines. Beside them stood a man in his eighties, leaning on his silver-headed walking stick. They all tried to ignore each other. Martti watched them absent-mindedly for a moment. The staff members moving behind the counter wondered at Martti's surprising appearance in this spot, since he had made a habit of staying put in his office during the day. Finally, Martti turned around to exit and started talking in a low voice to Head Pharmacist Liisa Laine, his employee of about ten years, who was standing beside him. She was usually the one tending to matters, according to Martti's instructions.

After a short negotiation, Liisa went to Anna, Pharmaceutical Assistant, acting as a scribe, and asked her to lock the pharmacy entrance door after the last customer. Anna was astounded by Liisa's request but agreed to obey as soon as the last customer was out of the door. She concentrated on finishing prescriptions waiting to be done at the same time as Liisa collected the drugs. Anna thought that something out of the ordinary was going on. It was the first time in her fifteen-year career at the Third that this had taken place.

After they had locked the doors, all the staff gathered in the storeroom in the middle of the facility for Martti's briefing. Sanna had chosen her seat as near to the back entrance of the room as possible. Martti spoke in a low voice about Mikael having an unlucky accident and all the imminent happenings after the police would arrive on the scene. At the beginning, Sanna's task was to lead them downstairs and cooperate with them. Sanna was able to see the shocked and unbelieving faces of her workmates. She could feel the tension growing moment by moment. Thoughts lashed back and forth.

Sanna had been widowed about ten years ago by a head-on collision with an oncoming car. She was the sole survivor of the collision, although badly hurt. Both her tibias were shattered. The operation was performed by Sanna's former colleague, Pasi Lampinen, who had been the second in command doctor on duty. He had completed it so well that Sanna had only scars to remind her of the accident. She had no recollection of the crash or the days following it. After a lengthy rehab, she had returned back to her pharmaceutical studies in Helsinki and had worked ever since, in partnership with Pasi's wife and her sister-in-law, Anu, in a well-established healthcare temp agency called Ex Tempore. Making the company into a success story had required a lot of work and time from them all. During the last couple of years, it had pulled its own weight. At the same time, Sanna's last intimate relationship had ended due to the guy leaving for Africa to build hospitals for the Red Cross. He never asked Sanna to join him, which suited Sanna perfectly well. After all this happening, an idea had planted in her mind to change her life. She had spun different scenarios in her mind, but only during the last couple of months had they revealed which direction she should make the change. While driving daily back and forth between Oulu and Pudasjärvi, she had had plenty of time to think what she wanted for her life. And on one rainy night, it had struck her. A sabbatical from all the work on the field would recharge her power altogether. She had invited her business partners to have a recreational girls' night out at her flat in order to tell them her decision. In addition to Sanna's revelation of the Big Bang, they had eaten well, drunk wine and watched both *Kill Bill* movies.

Sanna's sabbatical had not been a total surprise to the girls, as they had anticipated that something had been brewing in Sanna's mind for a while now. The change was supposed to happen by the turn of the year, when Sanna's temporary post at Third would end. Now, she wondered whether her anxiety had been a premonition of this. Sanna was overcome with a scary feeling that she was no longer in charge of her own life.

Luckily, Kristiina interrupted Sanna's thoughts by whispering to her: "Would you mind coming down with me? I thought that I could get the coffee gear from the coffee room up here, for example, to the scale room. The police can take their time to hustle downstairs in peace."

Once they got downstairs, Kristiina confessed that she wouldn't have dared to go there by herself. The very thought of Mikael lying in the spirits storage was an overpoweringly terrorising experience for her.

TWO

JUST AS THE TWOSOME had managed to arrange the coffee set-up on the countertops, the doorbell rang. With the two policemen in their blue overalls, came the Medical Examiner with his group. Sanna introduced herself to them, although she was already well-acquainted with the ME. Pasi Lampinen had made a career change from Surgeon to ME before Sanna's and Sami's accident. When the collision occurred, he had been standing in for his Orthopedic colleague in the operating theatre. Sanna realised that she hadn't had a proper conversation with Pasi after that. A high wall had risen between them and neither of them wanted to go over it.

"We were notified that there is a corpse in your spirits storage. Did you make the call?" Pasi looked at Sanna inquisitively. He saw how her whole essence oozed tension and realised that she was near collapsing.

"The apothecary called you after I told him of my finding. We agreed that I will show you the deceased and you can make your own conclusions based on that," Sanna spoke calmly and matter-of-factly, just like in the old days, working under pressure.

Sanna led the whole group down the staircase to the spirits storage door, opened the heavy fire door and turned on the lights.

As the door opened, Pasi took a step backwards, covering his nose and mouth when the musty, acid smell hit his nose.

Sanna passed him a small cardboard box full of oral masks.

Pasi grabbed one of them in order to cover his face from the smell. "You have quite a skanky aroma in there," Pasi stated.

"That fan up there has no strength to suck all the smell away. This is such an old house that they cannot manage to get proper air conditioning in." Sanna pointed at the air conditioner high up on the ceiling.

She turned the fire door to the maximum position in order to prevent the door from causing damage. The pump made the door swing shut even with the slightest movement.

Pasi pulled the protective gloves on and bent forwards to examine the corpse. He said to his assistant: "Take pictures of everything while I am proceeding so everything comes out in the right way."

He started his examination. Pasi's low voice making notes and his assistant's specifications were the only noises they heard for a moment.

Sanna made herself scarce quietly, into the coffee room. She felt a need for a breather before returning upstairs. She sat on the chair crosswise, her back leaning on the cool, stone wall. Mikael's waxy face floated on the retinas of her eyes at the same time as her thoughts circled around the incidents of the morning. She felt detached from everything. At this point, she didn't have the strength to sit in the scale room with the others, reminiscing about Mikael or contemplating what had happened.

Pasi emerged into the room and halted beside Sanna.

"Are you all right?" Pasi looked at Sanna anxiously.

"Still alive, unlike your patient over there." Sanna pointed her hand in the direction of the spirits storage.

"You are my patient, too, in a sense, anyway," Pasi sneered.

"There is no need to play doctors between us, since it all happened almost ten years ago. I just have to pull myself back together a bit before I return upstairs. The police are expecting some kind of statement, but I have no idea what to tell them."

"You just tell them what happened. You have given reports before, haven't you?"

"For you, it is easy to say. I feel like this is not real."

"Maybe it would be easier for you if you went upstairs to share some words with your workmates. We have to stay here for a while. By the way, Jaana told me about your new plans yesterday. Are you still going to pursue them?"

"Yes. However, I wish that I'd done it already. I said that I needed new challenges, but this is a little extreme."

"Well, I wish you all the best with that, if it is what you really want. I have to head back to continue my work. And you must be missed upstairs already."

Sanna stood up. She gave a slightly crooked smile to Pasi.

"So, just press your chin on your chest and proceed towards new disappointments," Sanna cracked.

Pasi laughed at her, shaking his head. "If that is your interpretation of what I just said."

Pasi returned to the crime scene and Sanna went upstairs. When approaching the scale room door, she heard Liisa reminiscing about Mikael and Sarita's wedding; she had been invited as a representative of the staff. Sanna snuck in the door, poured a cup of coffee and sat on the countertop to listen. She thought that it was good to hear others talking about Mikael, since it helped her to dissolve the flashing images of his dead face and bloody injuries.

When the conversation died, Sanna asked why Mikael had come to the pharmacy over the weekend. Liisa explained that their permanent cleaner was on sick leave due to her leg injury. Mikael had usually done his job on Friday evenings, but this week, nobody had seen him.

The conversation was interrupted by a noise, indicating a truck reversing out the back. The women looked around at each other with assessment.

Finally, Ritva stood up, sighed and said: "The goods are coming early today, I suppose. I'll go and take them in so we can sort them all out by the end of the day."

"Don't tell them anything, even if they ask why there are so many cars parked back there," Liisa directed her.

"Yes, yes! I'm not an idiot. I think the driver is too busy to notice anything, anyway."

THREE

INSPECTOR JUHO SEPPÄ SAT in his car with his working partner, detective Antti Virtanen. They had just taken a turn onto Church Street. They were looking for the gate leading to the back of the pharmacy. The place itself was a total mystery to both of them. They had thought they knew the locations of all the pharmacies in Oulu. On the way, they had contemplated the information received on the case. Constable Ville Koistinen had notified them by phoning Juho directly. The whole message made no sense, either to Juho or to Antti. Antti wanted to know who had made the discovery. Juho answered that one of the pharmacists had.

Just as Juho was about to turn to the wooden gate, he had to dodge a red and white truck across the road, getting ready to reverse through the gate.

Skilful driving, Juho thought when the truck slipped through the gate, the wing mirrors almost brushing the gateposts.

They followed it through the gate and parked their car in the same row, with others. Neither stepped out of their car before the truck driver had unloaded the boxes inside. Delivery was so quick that they had to hurry to get to the door before it was shut.

Inside the door stood a woman in her fifties, wearing a white smock, with scissors in her hand. She looked at the incomers suspiciously: "The pharmacy is closed now. The customers are supposed to come in from the front door."

The men introduced themselves and received a relieved smile.

"I am Ritva Halme, Pharmaceutical Assistant. The apothecary is in that office with the other police officers." Ritva pointed at a closed door beside the back door.

When they entered the office, they saw both constables bent over a computer screen, watching images, with a man in a white coat. The apothecary looked like they had expected: tall (at least six foot) and slim. His face was harsh and on top of his nose balanced metal-framed specs. Wavy grey hair was combed back from his forehead. Fatigue and sorrow shone on his face. He sat in a bent-down position as if his age was weighing him down.

Juho introduced himself and Antti and expressed his condolences. After a short briefing, they continued watching the video taken by the security cameras on the computer screen. They asked about the pharmacy's security protocol, and especially the layout of the security cameras. 'The girls' usually turned the alarm on, as well as closing the iron shutters on the back windows. Due to the quality of the cameras not being that great, the lad's face was not very visible. The timecode at the bottom of the screen showed Sunday at about 5pm. Finally, Martti sighed, took the CD out from the disc drive and put it into its case. Then, he sat on his work chair and asked the others to take a seat. Antti pulled a dictation machine from his pocket and asked if it was all right with the apothecary if he recorded the conversation. After a nod, he placed the turned-on recorder on the table. He named all the participants, as Juho started questioning. When Martti had told his version of events that morning, Sanna was asked to join in.

As Sanna emerged, Juho almost lost his breath in surprise. She was a spitting image of Juho's recent hungover morning's wet daydream: Nigella Lawson in her lilac-striped, white smock, hair pulled back in a French braid. She brought with her a tray full of coffee cups and a cup of sweet tea for Martti.

Sanna directed her attention to Juho and Antti. She reached out her hand to Juho and said: "Hi! I am Pharmacist Sanna Blinck. I gather you wanted to chat with me."

Juho took her hand: "I am detective inspector Juho Seppä and this is my partner, Antti Virtanen. My condolences on the demise of your workmate."

As Juho was expressing his words, he realised that he had said something utterly stupid. Sanna's smile had turned forced.

"Yes, of course, after all, that is… You seem to have advanced in your career. Last time we met, you had a different title."

There was irony in Sanna's deep, blue eyes, as if she wanted to know on what grounds the promotions were distributed. Juho felt an annoyance rising in the back of his mind, although her words were in no means offensive. Luckily, Antti had not noticed anything extraordinary in

Sanna's behaviour. Juho tried to shake off his irritation and focus on the problem at hand.

"My apologies, Mrs, or is it Miss Blinck? You said we have met before. Can you specify in what context it was?"

"You can just call me Sanna since it's easier that way. Our last meeting was ten years ago, after I had been in an accident, and you were supposed to take my statement. My face was bruised and swollen, so it's no wonder you can't remember me."

Sanna had sorrow in her voice as she continued on: "Actually, I didn't know Mikael that well as we never actually worked here at the same time."

"I will go to the pharmacy, so you can talk in peace." Martti stood up behind his desk and left the room, accompanied by two constables.

"Where do you want me to start?" Sanna sat down on a chair facing the sofa, where Juho and Antti were sitting. After finishing her coffee, she fumbled with the cup in her hands while waiting for the answer.

"Start from the beginning."

Sanna spoke peacefully, with a stolid face. Occasionally, she furrowed while trying to remember every detail concerning the issue. When the cup had diminished into a fingertip-sized blob, she threw it in the bin. She moved her hands to rub her knees, as if she needed to keep herself together. Eventually the conversation broke off. Juho and Antti tried to think of some specified questions, but Sanna's statement was so comprehensive that neither of them could come up with any. Instead, Juho asked Sanna to show them downstairs to meet Pasi.

Martti sat on a chair in the middle of the room, with a blonde woman in her forties. She got up to greet them.

"I am Liisa Laine, the head pharmacist. If there is something you need to know, don't be afraid to ask."

As they were descending the stairs, the rising smell started to strengthen. Juho tried to recognise it. The closest thing was the bitter odour of the paper mill, which hung occasionally over the town. They could also hear the medical examiners' subdued cursing and groaning. When they arrived at the storage door, Pasi threw them a spiteful gaze.

He scolded them for being delayed as he missed, according to his own words, the sweet smell of mortuary after this acid attack. Sanna watched his performance with amusement. She felt at home listening to Pasi commanding everybody around. It gave her reassurance that Pasi was in the lead.

When Pasi had said what he had to say to the policemen, he turned to Sanna: "Did you touch Mikael when you found him?"

"At first, I tried to shake his shoulder, then I touched his face. I wanted to know whether he was breathing. Then, I took a closer look with the flashlight."

"Can you show and tell us on the spot?"

Sanna nodded and grabbed disposable gloves from a shelf behind her back. At the door of the spirits storage, she knelt on the threshold while Juho and Pasi leant on the doorframes in order to follow her actions. She ducked forwards and adjusted her left hand between Mikael's side and arm. At the same time, she explained to the men standing in the doorway, her head turned upwards. When they had got a clear picture of the situation, Sanna stretched upwards from her tedious position. Just as she got up, she felt everything go dark in her eyes, and she started to fall. She stretched her arm and it hit something soft. She clenched her hand and held on, trying to get some air in her lungs.

Juho looked down when he felt a tight grasp on his shirt front.

Sanna staggered, with glassy eyes, her hand grabbing Juho's shirt.

Juho put his arms around her waist.

They stood there, interconnected for a moment, until Sanna shook her head and pulled away: "Sorry, I didn't mean to attack you. You can now let go of me; I suppose I can stand on my own."

Sanna flopped onto a stool, assuring everybody that she was all right. Kristiina emerged from the coffee room to witness Sanna's weak moment.

After making sure Sanna was okay, Kristiina joined Juho and Antti to give an interview in the coffee room.

"At what time did you come in here this morning?" Antti begun.

"I came around half past seven to open up the computers and get everything in order. They are always pharmaceutical assistant's tasks."

"How long were you alone in here?"

"Sanna came around eight thirty. Soon after that, everybody else was here. We do open at nine so that's when we all start our shift." Kristiina started to shake, and tears poured from her eyes: "Do you think the murderer could have still been in here when I came?"

They eyed each other.

Juho reassured the girl: "I don't think that guy wanted to spend the night here. Was the alarm on when you came in?"

"Of course, it was! The upper lock of the back door was not fastened, though. I thought that the last person leaving the premises had forgotten to secure it with a key."

"Who knew that Mikael was coming here on the weekend?"

"We all knew, except Sanna. And Mikael's wife, Sarita, probably some of his mates. It was no secret."

"How come Sanna didn't know? She works here as well, doesn't she?"

"This is Sanna's first day here. One of our pharmacists, Aune Kalliokoski, took a sick leave suddenly, last week. She was supposed to go on maternity leave, starting on the turn of the year, but she had some health problems due to her multiple pregnancies. Luckily, Sanna was able to come in at such short notice."

"Has Sanna been here prior to this or was this her first time?" Antti jumped in.

"As far as I know, she has been here before, doing temp jobs at least for a few years now. We call her company when it's urgent."

"Does that company have a name?"

"Ex Tempore Ltd."

"Thank you. I think we've got the essentials now. If something new comes up, you can call this number."

Juho dug a calling card from his pocket and gave it to Kristiina.

The threesome stood up at the same time and headed to the main part of the cellar. Pasi's group had already lifted Mikael's body onto a body bag, stretched in front of the storage door. Medical student Kalle Holopainen took a sneak peek inside to make sure that nothing was missed. All of a sudden, he bowed down and started to shoot something lying on the floor. It was a white, about twenty-five centimetre long club. Its other end widened into a half orb, stained with blood and hair.

"Can you tell us what this is and how it got here, Kristiina?"

"It is a pestle. You can find them in the lab in different sizes."

"Can we see the lab so we can get an overall picture of what can be found there? You can probably put that one in the evidence bag. Let's take it to be examined in the forensic lab," Antti said, and headed up the stairs.

The lab was situated at the other end of the rearmost storage room, opposite the apothecary's office. The room was a narrow space, left wall covered with kitchen cabinetry and a sink. Above the counter, there was a row of cupboards, looking like the ones used to keep dishes in. Beside the door, under the draining board, were drawer inserts, where Kristiina led them. She pulled out a deep drawer in the middle and showed pestles of different sizes stored in there. The smallest ones were made of stainless steel, but the bigger ones were all made of porcelain. She opened the other drawers, the top one containing spoons in different sizes, spatulas, scalpels and playing cards cut in half. Kristiina explained how they were used in the making of the pharmacy's Ex Tempore preparations. According to her, they used the playing cards for scraping the ointments and powders from the sides of the mortar to the bottom, for mixing things up.

The policemen chuckled at the fact that they had just learnt something new. The lab contained enough weapons to start a small village fight. On the back wall, there was a sterile cabinet that, at present, only contained a digital scale. They called Pasi's assistant to take some photos of the lab as well. The trio stood in the doorway, giving Kalle some space to complete his task. From their standing point, they saw Sanna and Pasi emerging through the door of Martti's office. Pasi lifted his black medical bag on top of the counter attached to the wall and opened it.

"I should have some emergency packages of diazepam in here. I'll give them to you just in case she needs them when you take her home. I don't think she'll have another panic attack, but if she does, you can handle that. How about you? Should I give you some as well, for the evening?"

"My darling, Pasi! Can't you remember what happened last time I took them? I was told I went ballistic." Sanna laughed at the old memories.

"Yes, now you mention it, I have some recollection of it. You were quite a spectacle back then. I thought that you would drop dead on the spot, but you were lucky to survive it."

Pasi glanced over Sanna's shoulder while he was talking and noticed the trio following the conversation. He directed his next words to Juho and Antti: "We have Mikael's wife, Sarita Liimatainen, inside the office. Martti told her the sad news and she had a panic attack. Fortunately, Sanna was there and she managed to calm her down. I have examined her, and you can go in there now, but I recommend that you let Sanna join you. I have requested that Sanna accompanies her home and makes sure she doesn't spend the night alone."

"Could you write down your orders for her own GP, should she need more medical help in the future?" Sanna asked Pasi.

Pasi nodded and headed to the office. A noise of a rattling keyboard went on for a minute and then Pasi returned with a piece of paper, which he passed on to Sanna to read before he folded it and put in into an envelope.

Juho wondered about the change in Pasi and Sanna's behaviour. In the cellar, Pasi had been in charge and Sanna had obeyed. Up here, they worked as equal partners. Sanna's intimate way of speaking indicated a longer cooperation, or even a closer relationship. Sanna tucked the envelope and the pack of tablets into her smock pocket before going back to the office. She left the door ajar. Pasi asked Kalle whether everything was ready for the removal of the corpse. Kalle told him that the porters already had Mikael on the gurney and they were bringing him up. After that, they started to go through the crime scene photos on the camera screen. When the picture of the pestle emerged on the screen, Pasi halted.

"This really looks like a murder weapon. It fits nicely into the lacerations on the head. The forensic examination has to be done, but I have no doubt this is the one."

"The thought occurred to us as well," Juho noted.

When the carriers reached the top of the stairs, they stopped to catch their breath before proceeding through the storage room to the back door.

They had reached the middle of the room, when a young, blonde, delicate-looking, crying girl barged out of the office. "Can I look at him for the last time before you take him away?"

Pasi nodded and moved to the head of the body bag to open it. Sarita looked at Mikael's face, tears in her eyes. She lifted her right hand, fore and middle fingers, pressed them on her lips first and then on Mikael's mouth.

Nobody moved or talked in the room. Juho watched Sanna, standing in the office doorway opposite him. Seeing her sorrowful gaze, he remembered their first encounter in the hospital. She had been so out of this world that he couldn't make head nor tail of what she was saying.

"You must be the policemen investigating this. I suppose we need to talk. I want Sanna to accompany me; I feel a bit queasy," Sarita said.

"That's quite all right with us," the men stated in unison.

They went to the office. Sanna and Sarita took a seat on the sofa below the window. Sarita started to tell them about her weekend with her parents in Rovaniemi. She had left there on Friday. On her return trip, she had tried to phone Mikael several times from the train. She had given up in the end and phoned Martti, who had asked her to come straight here. Her voice shook all the time, as if she was holding in a cry. Sanna sat quietly, holding Sarita's hand.

"By the way, did you find Mikael's backpack when you found him?" Sarita asked at the end.

Juho and Antti shook their heads.

"Maybe he has stashed it in his locker. Do you know where it is?" Juho looked at Sanna while talking.

"It must be up here. Martti keeps his stuff in that wardrobe, the one in the corner, over there." Sanna pointed her finger.

Antti opened the right-hand door. He saw white coats hanging there. Since the backpack was nowhere to be seen, he opened the other one. There were miscellaneous items on the shelves. On the top shelf, there were a couple of folded sheets, a blanket and a pillow.

"This might be a stupid question, but why are there bedclothes ready to use?" Antti enquired.

"In the old days, when all the pharmacies took turns being on-call, one week at a time one of the pharmacists would be on night duty. The bed was made ready for her, since she was allowed to sleep here when there were no customers," Sanna clarified to him.

At that point, Antti noticed Mikael's backpack on the bottom shelf. He bent over to pull it out and put it on the table to be examined thoroughly.

"You can tell us if the contents are intact so we can take it to the station," he said to Sarita.

Antti put the gloves on and started to empty it. Once it was done, Sarita pronounced that everything was there. Antti packed the things back in, along with Mikael's overcoat and shoes and gave Sarita a receipt.

"I think we can call it a day. I gather you ladies need a lift home," Juho suggested.

Sarita and Sanna agreed.

"As you know, Pasi ordered me to accompany Sarita home to look after her. He also asked me to give you these," Sanna noted as she dug the medical packages from her pocket and handed them to Sarita.

"These are supposed to be taken only when needed. If you have any feeling that you need more, you have to go and see your GP."

Sanna passed the envelope to Sarita, who opened it and read the contents. She tucked the paper into her purse, with the drugs.

"I'll have another chat with Martti and Liisa about tomorrow and then we can get you two home," Juho mentioned as he was leaving the room.

Sanna followed him to get changed downstairs.

"Sanna, before you leave, let's get you sorted with the alarm passwords. I'll let you know when we can open up next time," Liisa said to Sanna.

"Let's do it right away!"

They walked together to the alarm unit near the back door, where Sanna keyed her password in and saved it, following Liisa's orders. After that, Liisa conversed the next day's proceedings with Juho and Antti. She promised to be on site, although other members of staff were given a leave until further notice. Sanna went down the stairs to her locker to put on her civvies. This was the first time during the whole day when she had time to think about Sarita. In the back of her mind, she hoped that at least one of Sarita's friends could take charge of consoling her for the night. All Sanna wanted to do was to contemplate things over, in the privacy of her own home.

FOUR

AS SANNA RETURNED UPSTAIRS, everyone else was ready and waiting. Liisa asked Sanna to have a word with Martti before she left. She stayed there for couple of minutes, and when she came back, they heard her speaking about delivering the time sheets. The women squashed into the back seat, while the men sat in the front. As Juho asked for the driving instructions, Sarita told him to drive to Administrator Village in Linnanmaa. During the drive, Sarita told him that there was a third person living in their shared flat: Mikael's childhood friend, and his fellow student, Matias Lindström.

"Have you been in contact with him today?" Juho glimpsed through the rear-view mirror.

"I tried to call him, since I couldn't reach Mikke, but he never called me back, so I thought they were having a lecture or some other thing together."

"I don't think you should worry too much. Maybe his phone just died, or he has turned the sound off," Juho reassured her as they swerved into the courtyard of Virkakatu, number five.

Juho parked in front of the entrance, and they got out of the car.

As they were taking off their coats in the hallway, their attention was caught by a loud rhonchus, coming through a door opening to an open-plan kitchen. Sanna led Sarita straight to the living room. They sat on the sofa, leaving the policemen in charge of the snorer. The men went to Matias's room, but their efforts waking him up didn't pay off. Finally, Sanna went into the room after them to see if there was anything she could do to help them. Upon entering the room, there was a musty smell of old booze and the stench of a kebab. Juho and Antti tried to wake the sleeping youngster up, but he just curled deeper under his duvet. Sanna thought for a minute whether to let them continue their efforts or whether to put them out of their misery by interfering in the situation. Due to the fact that she just couldn't look at the fruitless efforts, she decided to cut in. She positioned herself at the head of the bed and lifted off the duvet in one motion from the top of the sleeper. With her other hand, she gripped his ear with her thumb and forefinger and twisted it. The exertion did its job. Matias bounced up with a roar and stayed swinging on the side of the bed.

"What the hell! Who are you?"

His eyes were off-centre, and he didn't seem to figure out what Juho was talking about.

"Do you think that having a cup of coffee would help the bloke sober up?" Juho asked Sanna.

She thought about it for a moment and then shook her head.

"Wait a second; I'll get you something."

They heard Sanna opening kitchen cupboards and the sound of a tap. When she came back, she was fiercely stirring a glass full of water and holding a big, plastic salad bowl under her arm. She handed the glass to Juho, saying: "Make him drink this as quickly as you can and do not take a hit."

She gave the bowl to Antti, telling him to be ready. After that, she backed to the doorway to monitor the situation. Juho started to pour the contents of the glass into the mouth of a protesting Matias, who let out a couple of loud burps after he had emptied the glass. Nothing seemed to happen for a while, until the muscles of his abdomen tightened and a huge geyser, smelling of beer and grilled food, erupted out of his mouth. Luckily, Antti caught most of the gush in the bowl. Juho's swerve was not quick enough, and part of the vomit splashed on his shirt. Apparently, Sanna knew what she was doing, since it had sobered Matias's head in one go.

Matias's face was still pale, his abdominal muscles still contracting, as if his body was still trying to get rid of something left over.

"Who is that crazy bitch and what the hell did she just make me drink? And who the hell are you?"

"I am Sanna, a nice nursing lady, who came to take care of Sarita. I made you drink stiff salted water so you can get better."

After Juho and Antti had introduced themselves, he asked: "Did you come here to arrest me? I didn't do it."

"Why should we arrest you?"

"Aleksi stole some rectified spirit from the lab. We drank it yesterday."

They explained the events that had taken place in the pharmacy to Matias. He buried his head in his hands and his shoulders started to shake with the power of crying.

"We were supposed to celebrate together after we finished an extensive written assignment. Mikael said he had to work for a couple of hours before he could join the festivities, and the rest of us went to Aleksi's place to start off. Everything went blank after that."

He lifted his head and asked: "Is it okay if I go and have a shower? It would clear my head. I am feeling a bit under the weather just now."

As he was given permission, he grabbed his towel and left the room. Juho followed him, with the full bowl. Having emptied it into the toilet bowl, he tried to clean the vomit stain from his shirt. He managed to get rid of it, but the smell kept lingering in Juho's nose.

When Juho came out of the toilet, he saw Sanna and Sarita sitting on the sofa side by side. Sanna had covered Sarita's nose and mouth with a paper bag. Sarita's breathing sounded laboured. Her chest pumped vigorously, as if she was suffocating. Her face was white as a sheet of paper, but the colour started to come back to her with every breath she took. Sanna's voice was very low when she repeated her instructions on Sarita's breathing. It was somewhat hypnotic, since Juho noticed that he started to rhythm his breathing to the same rate, with Sanna's calming voiced orders.

Eventually, Juho managed to tear himself away from the doorway. He shut the door and stepped into the kitchen. Sanna had apparently had time to brew a pot of coffee, so the men filled up their mugs. Matias joined in, after getting dressed. They went through Matias's account of the goings-on the previous day. Matias was very helpful, as far as he could remember, as to how the evening had gone. He also gave the contact information of his friends, Aleksi Raivio and Topi Koskela, and even let them study his phone voluntarily. It was very obvious that he still felt a little rubbery. Whether it was sorrow or the repercussion of boozing the previous night, it was hard to judge on Matias's appearance.

While they were finishing up with Matias, the doorbell rang. Sanna opened the door and led the comers straight to the living room. They heard two female voices, expressing their condolences. Sanna stayed in the kitchen. She pulled out a step stool, sat on it, poured a mug of coffee and looked out of the window, in a seemingly absentminded way. Juho watched her from his seat behind the dining table. Sanna turned her head, anticipating his gaze.

"Maybe I could head home; Sarita's friends can support her better than I ever could." Sanna threw her words into the air, as if she wasn't expecting an answer.

"Is it far? We can take you there by car if you need a lift," Antti answered on behalf of them both.

"Well, if it isn't too much trouble. I live in Meri-Toppila – it's within walking distance from here."

"No trouble at all! We're going the same way, anyway."

"I'll just say goodbye to Sarita and make sure she is coping." Sanna rose.

She squatted in the hallway to get something from her handbag. When she got up, there was a pen and a small piece of cardboard, the size of a calling card in her hand. After writing something on it, she went to the living room where they could hear sounds of conversation. In a minute, she returned to the kitchen.

"I'm ready now. I can wait if it takes you a little longer."

"I suppose we are quite finished here. We just need to ask Sarita if she knows Mikael's passwords on his computer. Or do you know them?" Antti asked Matias.

When he shook his head, Antti went to talk to Sarita. As he returned, he stuck his notes into his briefcase.

FIVE

WHEN THEY STARTED OFF, Juho asked Sanna's address.

"Sihtikuja, number one," Sanna answered.

"Is it that Sivakka house, just along Koskelantie?"

"No, it's the house behind it."

Juho continued driving in silence. Having to stop at the lights on the crossing of Koskelantie, he took a glance at Sanna on the back seat through the rear-view mirror. Her forehead was wrinkled, and her lips were moving as she was contemplating something in connection to the recent visit. Juho's sudden question startled Sanna: "What's bothering you?"

Sanna improved her posture.

"Those blokes got wasted for nothing."

"How come? Judging from his morning after, they had fun until the early hours."

"I don't see it that way. One is at the mortuary and the other one half alive at home. Things are not right. Something in Matias's demise seemed odd, but I can't put my finger on it."

"So, you don't think that they were too stupid to know their limits?"

"In my experience, a normal man has to keep quite a pace when drinking before he goes over the limit and his memory's gone. For a policeman, it can be a different ball game."

Sanna's words made the men burst into laughter.

"I have always thought of myself as being a normal man. How about the doctors? Do they have a separate classification?" Antti asked through his laughter.

"If you mean Pasi, he is a real pervert on his own account. He doesn't need booze for it. I must admit that it's been a while since we worked together."

"How did your cooperation come to an end?"

"It ended with a Big Bang, killing my husband. Pasi was the second in charge on-call Surgeon and operated on my broken tibias. Without him, my legs wouldn't reach the ground."

Juho jumped into the conversation: "As you said earlier, you have a recollection of me visiting you in the hospital."

"You are the first real memory I have of being in there; everything else is told by other people. Since then, my relationship with Pasi has gone sub-zero. Things got complicated due to my amnesia and his lack of understanding it."

Juho turned into Sellukatu, and Sanna gave driving instructions, until he stopped in front of staircase D and killed the engine. He turned to Sanna, asking what she had done the previous day. Sanna had taken her friends to their homes and returned in the afternoon. In the evening, she had talked on the phone with her mother between six and seven, but the time was irrelevant, since Pasi hadn't established the time of death so far. Juho made a dry statement that Pasi would gladly inform Sanna after the fact. Sanna couldn't help laughing at this; Pasi would never jeopardise the investigation by gossiping about the case to outsiders. Juho's facial expression told Sanna that he didn't believe a word she was saying. It irritated Sanna, and after giving them her calling card with her private number written on the back of it, she opened the door, before snapping: "Now, you boys can go and play nice with each other." She slammed the door behind her.

The men watched her exiting in silence. As she disappeared indoors, Juho started the car. The annoyance caused by Sanna's gaze in the morning, and her last words, caused Juho to erupt as he pulled out, making the gravel mixed in the snow fly behind the car. As soon as he was out of the yard, he hit the brake.

Antti looked at him wonderingly: "What is the matter? We are not in such a hurry that you have to go over grannies in order to get there."

"Sorry, that bitch's arrogant attitude started to bug me. First, she cracks a joke, and then gives us orders on how to do our policing jobs. I'm surprised she didn't give us a maternal tap on the head when telling us to play nice."

"I don't think that she meant anything by saying that, maybe she just wanted to get rid of us. I have to say that she is very quick-witted. It's difficult to keep up the pace with that one, that's for sure. All the answers come as quick as a shot."

"Ha, ha! No, do not start with this. Everybody is a comedian. Don't quit your day job just yet! She knew exactly what she was doing, every step of the way."

"Tell me about it! What was that collision thing at the pharmacy earlier? I somehow got the feeling that you two did not strike the right chord back then, either."

Juho thought about it for a moment. He recalled the rendezvous in the hospital years ago. He entered Sanna's hospital room, prepared with the data they had on the crash. Sanna had just been transferred from ICU to the ward. According to the information Juho was given, Sanna was conscious and able to answer questions. Once he first met Sanna, he started to wonder whether they had given all too bright a picture on Sanna's condition. She was somewhat scatty and watching the room door as if she was expecting somebody to come in. It was clear that she had no idea what the conversation was all about. In the end, Sanna started asking why he hadn't let Sami in to join the little chat, since he had let Juho in. After that, she closed her eyes and seemed to fall asleep. Juho left the room, frustrated. At the nurse's station, he got lucky; one of the consultants on the ward was there, studying his patient files before his rounds. According to his opinion, Sanna was still not oriented, neither time nor place. They had repeatedly told her about Sami's death, but the fact had not stuck in her memory. The doctor suspected it was due to a retrograde amnesia that caused the memory loss because she didn't have any recollection of the accident. The heavy pain relief medication might have added to her confusion. Juho had to be satisfied with the explanation, although it didn't take his frustration away. Ultimately, he confessed to Antti how the whole matter had bugged him ever since. When Sanna had reminded him about the whole affair, his reaction to it was more powerful than it should have been. Antti wondered at his mate's irritation; he usually had nerves of steel, even when things got tight.

During the conversation, they had arrived at the car park of the police house. Juho and Antti collected their gear quickly and headed upstairs to give their group a review of the situation. On their lift ride, they agreed to go straight into the big meeting room, where there were a couple of the movable whiteboards where they could arrange all of the gathered information so far. As they were walking towards the meeting room, Juho wondered why his workmates kept sneering at him when he passed them by.

Once they emerged into the room, Juho caught a glimpse of a picture hung on the whiteboard. In it, Juho stood in the door of the spirits storage, his hand on Sanna's waist. Her head was bent a little backwards, in a way that the only part of her face showing was the arch of her cheek. She had pressed her gloved hand on Juho's chest.

"Fuck, no!" he groaned, after seeing the picture and rushed to the board to rip it off. He crumpled the photo, before throwing it into the bin. Hearing Antti laughing behind his back made him more furious. Turning around, he saw Antti concentrated on the crime scene photos on the table, as if they were the only things that existed in the world. There was no point in rocking the boat about this, Juho sighed in his mind, but it explained the happy faces.

They spent the next hour examining the photos. The simultaneous walk through their notes helped them to put together a proper timeline on Mikael's activities the evening before. The crime scene photos were scattered on the table in order to give them a clearer picture of the body positioning and its surroundings. They picked up some of them to be hung on the boards as reminders. On the board, they also wrote names as they went along with their notes. When constables Antero Kokko and Ville Koistinen arrived with their coffee mugs to help them, they had already got off to a good start. The twosome had a bit of a curious look on their faces. Antti winked at Juho in order to warn him not to react to the prank their mates had tried to pull. Let them wrack their brains as to whether they had seen the picture or not. Juho took the hint and greeted them with a smile. Once he had a coffee mug in his hand, he began to explain how far they had got with the photos. Antero and Ville seemed disappointed, as Juho was focusing on the matter at hand.

Juho took the felt-tip pen and started to write names in order. The first name was Martti's, under it, the basics and the first interview conducted by Kokko and Koistinen. All the information they had gathered in the pharmacy was treated the same way. After getting everything down, Juho and Antti continued on the Linnanmaa events. Since this was new information, it took more time.

Ville had contacted the security company; they had Mikael's arrival and departure times in their journal. Or at least, the person using his password. The arrival time corresponded with Matias's statement, as well as the security camera's timestamp. His departure at 6.30pm put a time limit on Mikael's murder because it was obvious that he didn't set it. It raised the question: who was with Mikael in the pharmacy that night, and also, had they entered together or had somebody arrived later to do their deeds? In both cases, that person must have been somebody well-known to Mikael. He would not have let any strangers into the pharmacy after closing time. According to Matias's narrative, the three mates had been together all day and most of the night until early hours. The alibis of the rest of the staff were only partially confirmed. Juho told them that they had agreed to meet Liisa at the pharmacy in the morning at the same time as the forensic team was going to go through the spirits storage with a fine-tooth comb. Nobody was looking forward to finding anything new in there. All the staff members in the pharmacy had been there at some stage prior to the murder and left their marks in there. It was clear that the murderer had not stepped inside the storage. The fatal blow could easily have been given from standing outside.

While they were working, Antti picked up the photo of Sanna and Juho embracing from the dustbin and tucked it into his pocket. *Let them keep wondering what happened to it among themselves*, he thought. He just didn't want to be involved in any commotion. He bowed to the floor to pick up the forgotten backpack, belonging to Mikael. While emptying it, he listed out loud the contents, in the order they were on the table. They decided to take the computer to the forensic department right away so that they could have a closer look at it. His mobile phone and wallet were not found. Presumably, he had stashed them in his jeans' pockets.

They also decided to start interviews instantly after the autopsy. Ville and Antero focused on the staff interviews to start with. Juho and Antti would be talking to Mikael's friends and the family members.

As they were finishing up the day's work, their boss, Kyösti Raappana, emerged into the room to check up on their accomplishments. He asked about the photos on the whiteboard; the murder weapon caught his attention especially. After finishing his questioning, he turned to Juho: "Did you do more than one strip search while you were there or was that one enough?"

Juho was so dumbfounded at the question that he didn't come up with a proper answer. Luckily, Antti caught on fast and he was able to throw an answer: "Juho has such a flair with women that his pure presence on the spot sweeps them off their feet."

They all burst into laughter. When it died down, Juho explained the reason why Sanna had fainted. They had not realised that Kalle had captured the moment on his camera. In Juho's opinion, this was the perfect time to call it a day. They were all tired after the hard workday.

SIX

SANNA WAS STANDING INSIDE the basement door when the policemen accelerated out of the yard.

"And that's how you exclude Sanna Blinck from the investigation, not a single question as to her knowing what's what," Sanna muttered to herself, climbing up the stairs to the fourth floor. She went through the events of the whole day, trying to pin down the point where everything started to fall apart. It was obvious that something had set things off. A thing or two must have happened during the day to cause that. It had to be something that turned their attitude towards her. In Linnanmaa, she had talked mostly to Sarita, without getting a single question about it from the policemen.

Sanna had anticipated the drive home having a different outcome. After talking to Sarita, everything clicked, giving her new perspectives on this whole case. In the past, she could have discussed this with her husband or asked Pasi for advice, but now there was nobody and the policemen just couldn't care less. In the flat, she took off her outerwear.

Still deep in her thoughts, she went to the kitchen and made coffee, with sandwiches. Then, she sat on the living room sofa. TV on and attacking food, that would sort out the problem, for sure. An old recipe but one that had worked in the past. Just as she had finished her snack, her phone rang. She checked the caller: Jaana's name was on the screen. A good friend, she must have been talking to her husband Pasi about today's events.

"Hi! How's it hanging? You'll never guess who I met today at work!" Sanna responded, without waiting for the caller to identify themselves.

"Just let me handle my wife's hangings. Jaana already knows about our meeting today."

"Oh, it's you! I wasn't talking about you. How dare you call me after what you did!"

"What do you mean?"

"You put me in the same cab with those two keystone officers. You should have known that it was much about nothing."

"I am so sorry! I never realised there was a problem. You shouldn't have called me Darling at the pharmacy. How did Sarita cope in there?"

"Sarita got some friends to come over; they will keep her company until her parents manage the trip."

"That's good. I was just thinking if you'd be interested in assisting in the autopsy? We could have a proper chat about other stuff as well." Pasi tried to sound casual.

"Did Jaana put you up to it? I suppose I can come, since I haven't anything better to do tomorrow."

"I'll pick you up tomorrow at eight. See you then!"

After hanging up the phone, Sanna crossed her legs on the sofa. She didn't turn off the TV as she began yoga breathing to relieve her tension. She felt Juho's arms around her, and at once, her whole being relaxed. Although he infuriated her immensely, that hug gave her a sense of peace. Brief contact with him had felt improperly good in the moment. Sanna recollected all her dreams of him emerging by her bed. His presence had always felt good and safe. That had been enough for Sanna for the time being. And now, after a decade, Juho had popped up, although all her nearest ones had convinced her that his visit to the hospital had been just a hallucination. He was probably a family man, so this hug would never be repeated. In dreams, everything was still possible. After today, she was convinced that her decision to take a break from everything was the right one.

In the morning, Sanna stood waiting in the yard when Pasi pulled up in front of the entrance. He greeted her joyfully.

Sanna buckled up before she addressed Pasi: "You owe me an explanation about yesterday."

"What's that supposed to mean? Did Sarita give you hard time?"

Sanna gave an angry snort: "For the past years, all I have been to you is an unpaid nanny to your kids. All of a sudden, yesterday, I was an invaluable assistant to you, tending to Sarita. I haven't got a clue what's going on anymore."

"Jaana said the same thing last night. I have been a total jackass. I haven't realised that you've felt like an outsider. No wonder you need to take some time for yourself for a change."

"Is it really too much to ask? I just want my life back without all this baggage. I saw it more clearly with Sarita. She needed me more than anyone has for a long time." There was wistfulness in Sanna's voice. Sarita had totally needed her support the previous day. The ride home with Juho and Antti had almost ruined it. They had again made her feel persona non grata. In a different situation, Sanna could have verbalised to them all her own thoughts and suspicions, but it had come to nothing. Sanna looked slyly at Pasi, as he was contemplating his answer to Sanna's outburst. In her mind, Pasi had always resembled Mr Bean, both internally and externally. His clumsiness vanished only in theatre.

"How did they manage to get you so out of balance? Please, tell uncle Pasi everything, I may be able to help you."

Sanna reviewed what had happened between their arrival to Linnanmaa and her departure in Meri-Toppila. She followed Pasi's reactions during her revelation.

At first, Pasi mumbled compassionately, but as her story went on, his expression started to crack. He was able to contain himself until he pulled over to his parking space. Pasi turned off the engine and leant his head on his hands, resting on the wheel.

Sanna couldn't see his face, but judging from the jiggle of his upper body, he was laughing, with tears in his eyes.

Pasi was able to pull himself together slightly: "You are getting wicked in your old age."

Sanna frowned at Pasi, pretending to be angry with him, and then laughed at him: "I just couldn't stand their machoism. All they were interested in was showing off their superiority. The excessive amount of testosterone does that to you."

"I have worked quite a lot with them with no problems whatsoever. Usually, they handle things matter-of-factly, without any hassle. I must have a little talk with them after the obduction. Maybe you got it all wrong."

"What's the point? I am just a visitor here and you work with them on a regular basis. Tomorrow, they won't even remember me being there."

They got out of the car. Sanna followed Pasi's prompt pacing to the basement floor and up the stairs to the second floor.

In the middle of the long corridor, Pasi stopped at the armoire door. He dug a key from his trouser pocket and opened it: "You can get changed in there. My office is first on the left, behind those glass doors."

In Pasi's office, there were disorderly stacked bookshelves full of binders and trade literature. On the table, scattered around his computer, were piles of cardboard folders and papers. Pasi had got on similar blue scrubs as Sanna. Sanna sat on a chair opposite the table and put her handbag on the floor. She hung the key given to her by Pasi around her neck.

Pasi handed her Mikael's medical report. Sanna read the thin folder quickly. She looked up. Pasi browsed Sanna's actions from his side of the table.

"Is there something I should pay attention to?"

"We proceed the same way as we do with live patients. You can see from the papers his medical condition and then we'll see if our findings can support that. In case of giving a pre-op report, what are the things you point out?" Pasi was using his lecture voice.

"Relatively healthy young man. No operations prior to this. BP normal. As the bloodwork. Has gone through all the childhood diseases," Sanna listed by memory.

"Good girl! Now you can tell me what happened with Sarita. Did she tell you anything that seemed out of the ordinary to you?"

Sanna sighed and took a moment to think: "In my opinion, nothing. Sarita spoke mostly about what their life together was like. It was, in some parts, pretty personal stuff. I was not sure whether it went under the nurse-patient confidentiality or whether I should tell everything to the police."

"That's something only you can judge for yourself. As far as I know, the police have quite strict rules in that account."

"I gather we are both to blame. When I was talking with them, I was totally psyched. The way I handled things with Matias went very well, in my opinion. I had already started to create at least five conspiracy theories in my mind. Then, Juho asked me what I was thinking. I set out to talk about Matias, but those blokes weren't listening at all. After that, I realised how insignificant I was in their eyes."

Sanna's facial expression revealed how utterly disappointed she was.

"I totally understand why you are so unhappy. I can give them some feedback. Maybe it will make them more open to you." Pasi was as confident of his ability to make things right as he had always been when they had worked together.

"I don't want you three to get into a peeing competition. I'm here only on behalf of Sarita. She deserves to get answers and trusts me." Sanna wanted to make her position there clear. Pasi had a tendency to act in the most brisk way when he felt that someone had experienced injustice.

"Cross my heart and hope to die!" Pasi checked his watch. "Let's go downstairs so you can start the preparations with Kalle. I told the boys that we will start at ten. You can get all the preparations ready before that. I'll have to finish my paperwork up here."

Pasi collected his papers on the table. When Sanna got up from her chair, her at least one size too big scrubs waved around her slim body.

SEVEN

JUHO AND ANTTI WERE standing in the door of the autopsy room when they heard a low female voice saying: "Doctor, you should stop fiddling with your equipment. They have been laid there as you want them to be."

The men halted behind the door to listen to the doctor's comment, lifting their eyebrows at each other. Juho stated to Antti, almost silently: "As I told you, that woman pops up like a jack-in-the-box."

Antti laughed at him: "At least Pasi is not a Darling anymore. Maybe they've had a lovers' quarrel?"

"Let's go in and see what's going on in there."

Juho pushed the door open and uttered: "Good day! Are you all ready for the action?"

Then, he glanced in Sanna's direction. She sat on a high stool, leaning her back on the counter by the wall, her hands crossed over her stomach. Her eyes glimmered challengingly when they met his.

"How come you ended up in here? As I recall, you don't work here," Juho ejaculated.

"I told you yesterday that I am a working girl. It is mandatory to us needy widows to make a living by working our arses off. But what does a VVW like you know about that?"

"You don't seem that needy to me. What is a VVW? I'm asking just in case it comes up later."

"It's a man with a vacancy, a Volvo and a wife. Steady payment, domestic chores are taken care of and so on," Sanna snapped.

"In that case, I am just plain V, since I have neither a Volvo nor wife," Juho answered with the same tone. "So, I am the only one who doesn't tick all the boxes, aren't I, Pasi?" he continued with growing irritation.

"Leave me out of the big girl talks. My wife doesn't allow me to get involved. Which reminds me that I have to have a real man to man talk with the two of you. The nurse can come down here and earn her bread and butter. You two can stand wherever you want. If you feel faint, back off enough that you don't fall straight on the body."

Pasi's strict instructions got everybody to take their positions. At that point, Kalle entered the room with his camera equipment and took his place as well. Pasi clicked on the microphone hanging beside his head and began to dictate. After the case number, he continued: "Present Medical Examiner Pasi Lampinen, Staff Nurse Sanna Blinck, Medical Student Kalle Holopainen and Police Representatives Inspector Juho Seppä and Detective Antti Virtanen. Patient Mikael Liimatainen, age twenty-two…"

Pasi kept on dictating during the preliminary external examination. Once he had finished with the forepart of the body, and Kalle had taken photos of the parts Pasi had pointed out to him, he motioned Sanna to turn it around in order to examine the back. During the external examination, Pasi commentated on the meaning of every step. In his opinion, the lack of defensive traumas was a clear indication that at least the first blow was given to the back of the head.

"Sanna, can you tell me how somebody could blindside Mikael?"

"Even the slightest movement swings the door closed. If the perpetrator held the door, while Mikael was inside looking for something, all he had to do was to strike a blow."

There was nothing unusual about the autopsy. Pasi and Kalle stood on opposite sides of the table. Sanna was also near, standing beside the instrument table. She handed the instruments to the men on demand. Juho noticed that Pasi had no need to ask for anything he required. Sanna's eyes seemed to be all over the actions of Pasi and Kalle. At first, Juho had pondered what the little snapping sound he heard was every time Sanna handed over instruments, before realising that she did it on purpose. While Pasi dictated, Sanna made notes on a form attached to a clipboard. Occasionally, Pasi left Kalle to work alone, keeping an eye on his performance. He glanced at Sanna: "Have you ever thought of returning to proper jobs?"

Sanna looked back, her eyes glittering with laughter above her face mask: "And change my neat interior work to this? In here, all I have to do is give out and put in. Besides, I can push you doctors around out of the abundance of my heart."

"Do you seriously mean that drug dealing is more interesting than this?" Pasi frowned, pretending to be upset.

"That's what I am trying to explain to you. In here I just give, suck and spread, according to doctors' orders. In the pharmacy, I have a totally different impact on the results of my work. And it gives me the possibility to act straight with the customers. In an operating theatre, you never get a similar connection with the patients, due to them being half conscious on arrival." Sanna's whole essence showed her belief in her cause.

Pasi seemed to be satisfied with her answers and concentrated on the work at hand.

Juho had time to think about these people and the investigation while the obduction went on. They had spent the morning in the pharmacy, giving orders to the CSI team. Liisa Laine had been present, showing them the facilities more thoroughly than the previous day had made possible. She had classified the work roles of the different members of staff as well. Before finishing, she had given all the contact information of everyone for the interviews. When they had asked about the keys, she had pulled out a locked cash box containing bunches of keys and a small, blue school notebook, where she had all the names, dates and numbers of acquired and returned keys. They had also brought one of the pestles to Pasi for comparison.

Juho's thoughts were interrupted when Pasi pushed a big measuring cylinder under his nose, filled with yellowish fluid with floating bits, like vegetables in a soup. In Juho's mind, they looked like some grilled food leftovers.

"Does this smell like beer to you?" Pasi asked him, moving the cylinder into his hand.

"Yes, it does, at least to me. Why? Is it important?"

"I thought I smelled beer when I first opened the spirits storage door," Sanna stated seriously.

"How can you smell anything when the acidic aromas are so stiff," Juho wondered. "And why didn't you mention that yesterday when we were at the door?" he continued.

"I thought you smelled it, too."

Pasi put the lid on the jar and laid it on the table with the other specimens. He removed the organs, examined them and took all the tissue samples needed. Then, they packed everything back inside and Kalle stitched up the Y-incision.

They proceeded to the head. Sanna had shaved the hair around the blunt force traumas. Pasi asked Juho to give him the pestle as he began to compare it against the injuries both on the X-rays and on the sides of Mikael's head.

All of a sudden, he straightened, looked at Sanna and asked: "Can you show us how this is used in the right way? I just cannot figure out what the function of this is."

"Well, it is used for crushing and rubbing when we make tablet bulks. I can show you how it's done if you pass me one of the bowls behind your back."

Pasi passed her the bowl. Sanna took it, while continuing her explanation: "If you have a lumpy powder on the bottom, you crush them like this. After that, you rub the powder like this until it is pulverised. At the same time, you mix it this way." She made the movements for everyone to see.

The men had watched the presentation with interest, but nobody had any additional questions.

Pasi took the pestle again in his hands and tried to figure out the directions of the individual blows, varying his grip.

Sanna asked if it was possible that the first blow had been struck on the temple. When the victim was lying on the floor, he could have hammered him with the pestle to finish him off.

According to Pasi, that scenario could have been possible. The contusions on the brain, seen after they had opened the skull, fit perfectly with the external injuries. Finishing the whole autopsy, Pasi took off his protective clothing and gave orders on the preservation and handling of the samples to Sanna and Kalle.

"Sanna, have a break after you have tidied here. Kalle, you can start the lab works with the samples. I'll come to check them after I am finished with the boys."

He nodded in the direction of Juho and Antti. Juho felt like they were back in school, sitting in the front of the principal's office. Pasi's voice sounded harsh. Neither Juho nor Antti had any idea what the meeting was all about. Sanna concentrated on her tasks. Juho sensed some kind of resignation in her presence, as if she had something on her mind.

EIGHT

THE MEN SAT IN Pasi's cramped office. Pasi had placed himself behind his desk. Juho still had a feeling of being judged.

"That went well. I was a bit scared that Sanna had lost her grip altogether," Pasi sighed, relieved. He continued: "Sanna was really hitting it off today, agreed? Yesterday, she was getting up to speed quite slowly."

"I didn't notice any difference between yesterday and today." Juho shook his head. Antti nodded at his mate's comments.

"In Linnanmaa, she had full control of everything as far as I could tell. We were a bit horrified by the tough love she gave," Juho continued.

"When there is a life at stake, nobody expects anything less. What happened on the way home? Sanna was quite angry with you two last night," Pasi couldn't help but ask.

"Evidently, since she instantly phoned you. Is she going to make an official complaint or is this conversation enough?" There was annoyance in Juho's voice.

"Now, you've got it all wrong. I called Sanna. I wanted to know how Sarita was doing. I was also worried about Sanna's well-being. In my opinion, she was just picking up steam before you left."

"She could obviously hide it well enough. We had difficulties to keep up with her; she went on full steam ahead. We were just extras in that show," Antti defended as well as he could.

"Sanna is like Kipling's mongoose smelling a snake. Cannot stop when she gets a scent on something. She had managed to create at least five theories before you nixed her." Pasi had difficulty hiding his amusement.

"It is our job to contemplate the lines of inquiry, isn't it? We don't need outside experts doing it." Juho had become more and more irritated with Pasi's attitude towards Sanna. He had years of experience of those smart-arses, who had read detective stories from the cradle.

"Sanna had no intention of interfering with your job. It was more like wrapping everything up, as we do in the operating theatre after a difficult case. All she needed yesterday was at least some kind of feedback. Shooting down all her theories wouldn't have bothered her if you had just had the decency to hear her out."

Nevertheless, today, Sanna had made an impact on Juho. Usually, attending an autopsy gave Juho stomach cramps, but today, Sanna's pure presence had made him forget his feelings of nausea. His masculine ego wouldn't have allowed him to lose his nerves in front of a female.

All of a sudden, a memory of Sanna fainting the previous day popped up into his mind. Would Sanna have done the same thing in the case of obduction fumes sweeping him off his feet? He found the thought amusing for some reason because Sanna was so much smaller than heavyset Juho. Nevertheless, Juho had a hunch that Sanna would at least try to prevent his fall. Then, as a continuum to his thoughts, he saw through his mind's eye, while Sanna was sorting the used instruments and bending forwards over the basket on a roller table, her scrubs top slightly slip down, so he had good visibility of her bra. The vision lasted only a few seconds before Sanna pulled it back. It almost knocked him down.

"I suppose we have to take the initiative and clean the slate." Juho dug his mobile phone and Sanna's calling card out of his pocket as he was speaking.

"Should I call her work or private number?" he pondered out loud.

"Use the private one. Sanna is more likely to answer that one," Pasi answered.

Sanna had managed to camp comfortably in the corner table of the coffee room when her phone rang. Juho's voice sounded a little apologetic.

"Hi, this is Juho speaking. Why don't we have a little chat to sort things out?"

Sanna smiled inside as she answered: "That suits me very well. Your place or mine?"

"If my place means the police station, it suits me. We can take an official statement at the same time. We'll wait here at Pasi's office until you are ready to leave."

"Okay! I won't be long. I'll just change and put my civvies on. Bye-bye!" Sanna emptied her coffee cup, collected her things and rushed to the linen room.

On the drive from Oulu University Hospital to the police house, Sanna kept on a light conversation of anything but the murder case. Luckily, Juho and Antti joined in her chatting.

At the police house, Juho and Antti led Sanna into an imposing space, a small meeting room. Walking down the corridor, she felt inquisitive looks thrown in her direction. It amused her. In the meeting room, Sanna took off her coat and hung it on the back of a chair. She took a seat next to it. Juho asked if Sanna wanted a cup of coffee.

She said yes: "Black coffee, please. No sugar."

Juho had printed Sanna's statement from the previous day. They went through it, page by page. Juho wrote all the changes straight on his computer. After completing their task, Sanna suggested a toilet break. Antti left to guide her there and promised to bring more coffee on the way back. Juho stayed put, scrutinising the statement. He was so focused on his work that he didn't notice the time. The smell of fresh coffee distracted his attention.

"Have you lost Sanna?" Juho pried.

"What! Isn't she back yet? It took me a while; I had to make some new coffee since the pot was empty," Antti pondered.

"We have to go and make sure that she hasn't fainted again."

They both knocked on the locked toilet door. Sanna's voice was subdued when she answered: "Don't worry; I'll be out in a jiffy."

The door opened and Sanna exited, looking radiant. Her cheeks were burning red, and her eyes shone with laughter: "Sorry, I lost track of time. I needed to collect my thoughts."

"Are you sure you're okay?" Juho asked anxiously.

"I haven't made a habit of fainting; yesterday was an isolated incident. I have a low blood pressure. When I get up too quickly, it makes me pass out. It is called orthostatic dizziness. In the morning, I fell flat on my bottom when I discovered Mikael's body for the first time. I didn't want to have an encore in front of everyone," Sanna explained.

"Tell me about it. I printed your new statement while waiting. We need you to read and sign it so we can proceed." Juho handed the papers to Sanna.

Sanna did as she was told.

"Are we finished now?" Sanna had hope in her voice.

"Are we keeping you from something? We haven't talked about that gig in Linnanmaa yet. Pasi mentioned that you had at least five different theories hatching yesterday," Antti joined in.

"Well, well. Did Pasi really tell you that?" Sanna smiled back. What else might he have said before they got their swords out, Sanna wondered silently. Out loud, she said: "After the obduction, there were only three left. Two of them went straight down the drain after the tests were taken."

The men took a quick peek at each other. This was getting interesting.

"What went wrong?" Antti continued.

"I made my conclusion in haste. It was unbelievably daft of me, thinking that he had brought his lover boy to live under the same roof with his wife. Fortunately, during the autopsy, the thought vanished into thin air. Same thing happened with the possible fancy woman on the side," Sanna commenced uncomfortably.

"How did you come up with that conclusion?"

"There were no external indications supporting it. Ergo, no fluids or anything else," Sanna went on.

"Did Sarita tell you that Matias is gay?" Antti jumped in.

"Is this some kind of trick question? You two have eyes, don't you? It is out in the open if you just know where to look. It has no bearing in this case, anyway. The boys have known each other since they were lads. Or that is what I gathered." Sanna was amazed at how slow those two were. Maybe they thought it so meaningless that it would be a waste of time to pay any attention to it in her presence.

"What got you to think about that? Did Sarita imply something was up?" Antti pressured.

Sanna was deep in her thoughts, frowning her eyebrows: "Sarita told me they'd been having some sort of heated conversations since last spring. Mikael was concerned about something, maybe even a bit scared. Matias moved in all of a sudden, without speaking with Sarita at any point. I also thought that the voicemails Mikael left were somewhat cautious. As if he didn't dare tell her everything. He just promised to come clean when Sarita returned home. Matias conducted himself rather strangely. Of course, he lied about almost everything. People lie to you all the time, anyway, but you have got used to it, being policemen, I mean."

Sanna was a little out of breath finishing her speech.

"How did you know he was lying?"

"I really cannot say. I got a sort of tingle when he spoke about the Sunday evening. I just always know when somebody is making shit up," Sanna tried to explain her vibes. She had tried to analyse it but had never been able to get to the bottom of it.

"Did you get the same tingle with Sarita?" Antti wanted to make sure.

"No, I didn't. But it was a totally different situation. I just listened to her talking. I was there to console her, not to fish for information. Sarita relied on my professional secrecy in all our talks. Same applies to you, according to Pasi." Sanna's smile to the men was a little crooked on the last sentence.

"Why don't we get back to your theories again. You said about having at least five of them, minus two. What were the three others?" Antti went back to the earlier issues.

"One of them was in connection to that threesome. Maybe a student prank went too far. That stolen spirit might have been part of it. The two other ones are connected with the pharmacy action. There is a possibility that someone had done a thing or two in the past, finding a way to cut in on the profit. Or built a drug plant on their inherited abandoned farm. These last two are purely products of my vivid imagination. There are no grounds to support them." Sanna ended her outburst with a sigh.

She sensed their disregard. Juho's next words verified the fact.

"We are in the habit of finding the facts and proceeding with those investigative lines. For the sake of your own safety, you should leave all the inquires to us. If you find important clues, please do contact us before you do something you will regret." Juho tried to sound determined and convincing.

"Let's have a word about Matias. Do you always treat your patients with such tough love?" Antti tried to defuse the situation.

"Of course not! It is usually just to use on doctors!" Sanna had a semi-smile on the corners of her mouth when replying.

"I see. Why only on doctors?"

"They work long on-call shifts, sometimes up to thirty hours non-stop. Only time they can have a rest is when the ward is quiet. Some of them sleep like logs, so in case of an emergency, they have to be woken up quickly and effectively."

"Why did you give him the stiff salted water?"

"I thought at least it wouldn't harm him. I had no idea what kind of mixed substances he had taken during the evening." Sanna looked straight into Antti's eyes.

"Were there signs in him that indicated something else other than alcohol overdose?"

"He was so fucked-up, and there were other signs as well. I just cannot put my finger on it. It still bothered me after I got home," Sanna frowned, annoyed.

"Let us know when you figure it out. It could be useful to us." Antti ended the conversation on his part. He nodded to Juho in order to let him continue with the talking. He couldn't come up with anything.

Sanna was also looking knackered, rubbing her knees and rolling her shoulders.

"I suppose we went through the most important parts; in other words, we can call it a day," Juho said and turned off the recorder.

Sanna took her coat and started to put it on. While she was muffling her woollen scarf around her head, Juho also stood up.

Having adjusted her scarf, she turned to Antti: "Can you send your number to me? I have Juho's already saved on my phone."

Antti nodded at her, smiling. Juho said, tensely: "I'll take you down. Can you catch a bus, or should I give you a lift?"

"It's okay if you just show me the way out. With my sense of direction, I might be looking for the exit until tomorrow. I know how to get home on a bus, since it gives me a chance to stretch my legs a bit. Being an elderly lady, my joints tend to stiffen when sitting a while in one position."

They started to walk together along the corridor, towards the lift.

"You don't give me much credit, do you?" Juho stated seriously, as they reached the lift door.

At the same time, the lift door opened and a man on his fifties emerged.

Sanna paid no attention to him, saying: "Juho, listen, you are such a cuddler and probably very good at what you do. But the existential crises of needy widows are not a part of your skill set."

The man exiting the lift gave a prolonged look at Juho when he let Sanna go in first. He was annoyed due to the fact that he realised Kyösti had heard Sanna's speech. He felt a blush emerge on his face. Somehow, Sanna always had a way of keeping him on his toes, whatever he tried to do. Sanna looked at him and saw his embarrassment.

"Sorry, I didn't mean to make you look bad in front of your colleagues."

"I suppose he has heard far worse things around here. Have we upset you? Where did that last remark come from?"

"I am not upset. On the contrary, your double act is enough to make anybody's day. It took me a while to get it. That's why I had to stay in the powder room so long. It was very difficult for me to keep a straight face after that."

"What act? We are just trying to get our job done."

"Sure thing. It must work better in a bar. You just keep up that Joe Cool look and Antti as your wingman. You leave us women no choice but to surrender."

"And who might that Joe Cool character be?"

"He is one of the alter egos of Snoopy from *Peanuts*. He also has a wingman: a bird called Woodstock."

Juho started to laugh at the allegory Sanna had just painted.

"How does this affect our work? That was the thing you commented on."

"Your double act is pulled together so well that nobody else can squeeze in. Tomorrow, you will have forgotten even my name and everything I said today."

They had landed in the basement. Sanna reached out her hand to Juho before she exited through the door. Turning back, Sanna waved her hand, saying: "I'll be back!"

Juho took a moment, contemplating. He thought about Sanna's last words. She might have a point. He returned to the office. Kyösti, who was standing in the doorway, cracked: "There's our cuddler coming back from escorting the widow."

Kyösti exited, chuckling. Antti looked at Juho, saying: "Did you get spanked by Sanna?"

"No more than a clear picture of my job description and intellectual capability."

His statement awoke Antti's interest, so Juho had to report their conversation in the lift to him.

"Now I know why you are still a bachelor. That kind of pocket Venus almost offers herself to you and you still have no clue. Or are you telling me that your thing-a-ding didn't ring-a-ding at all, even when you were holding her so close?"

"I'm not made of wood, you know. And Sanna has no need to reveal more – I have seen the whole thing."

"Where exactly?"

"Just after the autopsy. Sanna was sorting the instruments into the baskets. She happened to bend down, and her top dropped so conveniently. I don't think that Sanna realised that I saw everything."

"Tell me more; this is getting interesting. What did your experienced investigator's eyes see? I'm just asking because I want to learn from the best."

Juho burst into laughter: "I don't even know what to say. Figuratively speaking she is quite well-rounded."

"So is the statue of Market Police in the seaside market square."

"I was thinking more like the one we saw at the Big Church. Then we sang a serenade of 'Sex Bomb'…"

"Oh, you mean Miss Manta from the Big Church," Antti chuckled.

He recollected their pick-up gig in Helsinki the previous spring. The colleagues had been overexcited to offer the boys from the north a long-version tour around the capital. They started off wining and dining in Mamma Rosa. After dinner, they were taken to the Police Hut seaside sauna in Lauttasaari to get a proper steam boil.

During the evening, the whole bunch decided to continue on their tour of the city; their colleagues wanted to show them their most popular watering holes. At some point, they had begun to compare the best tourist attractions in their hometowns. According to the Helsinki residents, their Havis Amanda on the market square had no real opponents anywhere. Accordingly, they walked as one down to the market square to validate it. Juho and Antti were obliged to admit the maiden attracted the eye more than Oulu's own landmark, Market Police. Honouring the damsel, they were set on a serenade. The only appropriate song coming into their minds was Tom Jones's hit song 'Sex Bomb'. On return to Oulu, they had been slightly embarrassed by their enthusiasm.

"Could you specify, just for professional development purposes, whether Sanna's rack was all natural, or was there a little bit of filling put in?"

"All natural, definitely. You can tell how they fight to be free. You should know that much, being a married man and all."

"You are really a man with principle. Work first and then fun, even when somebody offers you sweets on a silver plate." Antti couldn't help himself, picking on his mate.

He continued in connection with the day's work: "We should have a brainstorm before we call it a day and collect all the data so we can start off the interviews tomorrow."

"That's the best idea you've had all day. And could we please concentrate on the other ladies from now on? We will spend the rest of the week having a proper talk with each and every one," Juho sounded a bit impatient.

They focused on gathering together every bit of information chronologically. Once they were ready, they moved to the meeting room and updated the board for the follow-up.

NINE

IN THE MORNING, ALL four of them began to scrutinise the autopsy report Pasi had provided them with. Ville and Antero were interested in their account of the events from the previous day. Especially Juho's demonstration of the proper usage of the pestle, which was new information to them. The forensic team had also finished their investigation. They hadn't been able to retrieve any beer cans or fast food packages. Mikael had obviously enjoyed his last meal before entering the pharmacy. They had to find out whether he had eaten alone and where he had done it. Antti phoned the lads. They might be able to verify Mikael's timetable on Sunday. They got lucky; Topi answered that he was just returning from Linnanmaa with Aleksi. They agreed to come straight away so that things could be sorted out immediately.

When they were arrived at the police station, Juho met them downstairs. As he was shaking their hands, Juho assessed them quickly. Topi's appearance startled him due to the fact that he could easily be Mikael's brother. The half-length blondish hair, blue eyes and slim build were the same. Aleksi, on the other hand, was dark-haired and brown-eyed, more heavily built than his friends. Both boys had typical attire on: jeans, trainers, hoodies, woollen hats and backpacks.

For the interviews, Juho and Ville took Topi and Antti and Antero took Aleksi. Juho led Topi straight to the interview room. He asked Topi about his friendship with Mikael. According to Topi, they had been in the same lab team since the beginning of their studies. They bonded and formed a close friendship and did most of their group work together. In the week prior to this, they had worked long hours in the lab, analysing drugs in regard to their pharmacological course. They had got the results on Friday and spent the whole weekend writing their report. It had taken all day Saturday and Sunday, so they had agreed to have a boys' night out as soon as the report was complete. They had left the Med School library around four. Topi and Matias had stayed in Aleksi's flat in order to get the evening going. He had no recollection of what happened during the rest of the night. He had woken up in some pussy's bed. He had gone home in the afternoon. And then Matias had phoned him. Topi had gone to pieces once he heard the news.

Juho listened to Topi. His speech was clear and convincing – he looked into his eyes and sat up straight in his chair. Under the surface glimmered hidden anxiety. His statement was similar to Matias's due to them being able to make their stories fit. Juho reminded himself of Sanna's suspicions of the choice of substances they had taken. On the other hand, all that Topi was ready to admit was that they were boozing heavily that night. They had a zero-tolerance policy on drugs.

In order to change the subject, Topi went on inquisitively, asking where Mikael had been found and who found him. Juho replied that one of the staff members did the finding. Topi asked if the finder was a curvy brunette. As Juho ducked the question, Topi confessed that he had been in a club, Utopia, a few months prior, with Mikael. There, they saw a slim, curvy brunette in her thirties, and Mikael told him that the female in question had worked in his father's pharmacy over the summer for a short period. Then, he had revealed her status of being a big player in drug trafficking. According to Mikael, she sold really high-end stuff. And if you wanted to get laid, that could be arranged. Topi said he had thought that Mikael was telling him a cock and bull story. He couldn't remember her last name, but he thought the first name started with S.

Juho made an excuse and announced a short break. He exited the room and texted Antti to meet him in the corridor. They had a short chat before they returned to carry on with their interviews.

During Topi's story, Juho's thoughts went to and fro. Upon first hearing his story, it sounded truthful, but there was something in it that rang a bell. He contemplated Sanna's behaviour; he had no idea how her mind worked. Anyway, Topi's telltale made no sense to Juho. He couldn't understand why Topi wanted to pull Sanna in this early on the case.

Talking about his studies got Topi really excited. He began to paint a picture of intelligent, fierce, best of the best fighting over the highest grades and rankings. All that hard work required heavy fun to balance it out. For Topi, this was a whole new world, since he had spent most of his life in the small circles of Haapavesi, where everybody knew you. His parents had a beef cattle ranch; they wished for an easier life for their only son. He had never wanted to be in the family business. At some point, Topi had a dream of becoming a vet, but treating people was a more appealing option to him in the long run. Especially since there was a Med School in Oulu, near his home. Juho started to feel like Topi could rant on and on about his superiority all night long unless he could somehow make him stop. In order to change the subject, Juho aroused questions on Topi's girlfriends, former and present. This line of questions made Topi seemingly uneasy and gave Juho a good excuse to end the interview.

After that, Juho and Antti compared their notes on the lads' comings and goings on Sunday. When they realised that both stories were similar, word for word, they decided to speak with Matias. Maybe he would remember things differently this time.

Aleksi had told them about being from Rovaniemi; his father was a GP in a local health centre and his mother a manager of an old people's home. He had known Sarita only by face until Mikael had started dating her. Mikael had never mentioned to Aleksi anything weighing on his mind.

Nothing worth mentioning had come up when talking to Liisa and other staff members. Every one of them had spent a casual weekend. According to them, Mikael was a nice and ordinary family boy with a bright future awaiting him.

Antti contemplated Sanna mentioning that Mikael had been worrying about something. He phoned Antero to ask if the forensic team had made any progress on Mikael's computer. They had only been able to have a cursory look the previous day. Probably, they had already found something enlightening on the issue. Antero said that he hadn't been notified of anything special; most of his files seemed to be a part of his studies.

TEN

SANNA'S FIRST INTENTION LEAVING the police house was to walk straight to the nearest bus stop, but her growling belly made her change course to the citymarket store across the street. Wandering down the shop aisles, she contemplated her feelings and fretted to herself; how stupid she had been, hoping that Juho might ask her to dinner to cheer her up. On the other hand, she was happy about him not figuring out her attempt. Sanna swore that this would be the last time she tried anything of the sort involving Juho. She should waste no more sentiments on a blockhead like him. It was a pity that she had nothing but empty days ahead of her, only her own thoughts to keep her company.

At home, she decided to leave all futile yearnings behind her and focus on her own issues. There were Sarita's matters to attend to at some point, but it was all up to her. Probably, it would take some time, since it was Sarita's own business to phone her when she needed her services. Nevertheless, she had made a promise to Martti to take care of Sarita, as a paid employee, whenever she required her assistance. Today was her time to look after herself. It was meant for her to empty her head, accompanied by *The Bold and The Beautiful* and *The Hidden Lives*.

Before that, she decided to make notes on all this. She went to her study, where she always used her desktop computer for work. It felt more official. At the same time, she sent emails to her associates. They must have read in the newspapers about the happenings of the previous day, but she wanted them to know what the real situation was. After finishing work, she made a call to her brother, Alpo, just to get some consolation. She didn't give any details about her discussions with the police or relating to the murder, although her brother tried to pry, beating around the bush. Sanna dismissed the unhappy affair by pleading confidentiality; she had no desire to talk about it anymore.

The next morning, after breakfast, Sanna went up to town to visit the library, where she hadn't been for a while. She went to the borrowing department and, later on, spent time in the Journal Hall, going through all the women's magazines she never bothered to obtain. The crown of the day was a coffee with a pastry in the Library Café.

Minutes after Sanna got home, her phone rang. The caller was Anu, Sanna's sister-in-law and associate at Ex Tempore. Anu enquired about Sanna's schedule as she wanted company on her afternoon coffee break. Sanna replied with joy; Anu's company was just what she needed on a day like this. They agreed to see each other in an hour, after Anu had called it a day.

When the doorbell rang, she was surprised to see both her associates. They brought plenty of Hai Long's best delicacies in takeaway boxes and a few wine bottles to flush the food down with.

"We are holding an extra-corporate meeting and enquiring as to what you have been up to recently," Jaana bellowed, after giving Sanna a long hug in the hallway.

"So, you two wanted to ambush me, making sure I was home alone?" Sanna laughed, pleased by her friend's surprise. "We should enjoy our meal first so we will have strength to go through our agenda before you two have to sign in at the barracks," Sanna went on, with a broad smile on her face.

"Well, we've got a proper night off from the company. Our hubbies are taking care of the children. We said that we have to be on the move, in need of a surprise attack on you," Jaana declared as she was setting the food boxes, plates, glasses and cutlery on the table.

Sanna sat, enjoying her friends' joyful laughter, while Jaana and Anu took care of the drinks. Their joy was contagious, as the table was filling up with yummies.

"Let's eat in peace and decline to talk business until all the food is gone," Anu stated with enthusiasm, sniffing the food.

They shifted to the living room after their meal to enjoy dessert coffees with wine. Once they were seated comfortably, Jaana declared: "Sanna, this is really an intervention. We are anxious to hear everything about that sexy policeman of yours. And all the dirty details, please, please!"

"When did you have the chance to check out his handsomeness, established wife and mother, my friend?" Sanna wondered.

"Even a married woman has to have her eyes wide open when the opportunity strikes. And the guy is Lilja Eriksson's former boyfriend, I mean, until Lilja ran off to the States with Jarkko Järvenpää. The ones left mourning were his wifey and two children, together with Juho. I met him when Pasi and I went to Lilja's after-party, held on the evening of her defending her doctorate. We all drooled with envy when Lilja sailed in with a hunk like that. If you can imagine Danny Messer i.e. Carmine Giovinazzio with a Finnish twist, you'll stop wondering what we are talking about," Jaana bragged.

"He also happened to be that policeman who came to interview me at the hospital. The one who was supposed to be my 'dream man'," Sanna continued the story.

"Now you are pulling my leg, nobody but you saw him in there. He really does exist, doesn't he?" Jaana went on for the both of them.

They had never really believed Sanna's story of the policeman visiting her room. That was why they had started to call him Sanna's 'dream man'. Over the years, they had teased Sanna for hallucinating, seeing Sami beside her hospital bed after his death. Her friends had been able to convince her that Juho's visit belonged to the same category. Sanna had never dared to admit to her friends that Juho had appeared in her dreams several times since then. It would have ascertained to the girls him being just an illusion. She could never admit to them how much Juho's appearing in the pharmacy had upset her.

Later on, the girls began to enquire about Sanna's visit to the police station. They wanted to know if the interview had gone on with the same kind of distortion as in the obduction room. Sanna told them that they'd had a good-spirited conversation. On the other hand, when she told them about the chat she and Juho had in the lift, Anu and Jaana laughed their arses off. They told her that she should have got straight to the point and not taken the scenic route into a man's pants. Sanna admitted they were right. Juho would have been a good candidate for giving her unproven princess bed a good test ride.

This subject would have gone on forever, but Jaana and Anu were quite keen on something more exciting happening, that is Mikael's murder and the things connected to it. Neither had any experience of the murder investigation. They wanted Sanna to conduct a full summary of the case. Jaana complained how reticent Pasi was about his work and belittled the attraction. In his words, it was mostly checking out death certificates and other paperwork. It was almost miraculous that he mentioned seeing Sanna at the crime scene.

It took nearly an hour for Sanna to explain everything that had happened in the pharmacy and afterwards. She apologised to her friends, remembering Juho's warnings not to mix herself up in any more of the investigation.

Anu stated that in these circumstances, Sanna had a front row seat doing her own, unofficial enquiries on the matter. And in case she did find out something connected to it, she should inform the investigators immediately. After all, Sanna had contact with both the pharmacy staff and Sarita. Through Sarita, she could also meet the boys in a more relaxed environment. They had all experienced that it was easier for people to share their deepest concerns with a nurse than a doctor, let alone the police.

They closed the case after resolving the issue.

ELEVEN

SANNA INTENDED TO USE the rest of the week to sort out the facts. She wanted to take time to go through all the events so far. Soon after her friends had left, she began to list all the matters she needed to attend to. On that same file, she made a timeline and wrote down all the questions she needed answers to before she could proceed.

Sarita's hysterical call interrupted her working. She had received Mikael's death certificate and had no idea what she was supposed to do with it. Sanna printed her to-do list on the matters they had to deal with. Going through the whole list would take several days due to having to fill in a myriad of different kinds of forms. Sanna had a vivid image of her own experience on the quantity of papers linked to a death.

In Linnanmaa, only Sarita and Matias were there when she arrived. Sarita's parents had gone back to Rovaniemi to get things sorted. Sarita told that her they were coming back the next day. Martti had invited them to stay over as long as they needed. Matias was slightly embarrassed of his behaviour on the day they last met. Sanna understood his shamefacedness, although she wasn't quite sure how sincere he was. One possibility was that he felt guilty for having fun, while his friend was being attacked. A guilt trip made people behave peculiarly.

Sanna apologised for her brutality on that day. She explained having to make sure his condition was not life threatening, since she had no idea what the boys had taken.

Matias understood her account. He denied ever taking anything stronger than ibuprofen. On Sunday night, they had wanted to celebrate completion of a large study report. It determined the score of the whole course and none of them wanted to fail. They had worked their arses off the whole week. Even Mikael had taken a day off on Friday, making arrangements with his father to go on Sunday instead. The other three had stayed in Aleksi's flat in Hallituskatu, starting off the evening when Mikael had left for work. Matias was annoyed about his blackout. He had only a few scattered flashbacks of them drinking rectified spirits Aleksi had stolen from the lab and eating sausages and chips at some point during the evening. He had no memory of coming home. Obviously, he had ridden his bike; it was at its normal place under the front porch canopy. The most annoying thing was that he hadn't been able to support Mikael in his hour of need, as he had done for him when he had had a really bad break-up with his partner. Mikael and Sarita had offered to take him in and support him. All of a sudden, Matias was awoken to the fact that Sarita and Sanna might have some one-on-one things to tend to. He offered to go out to give them time to chat in peace, but Sanna rejected the offer –

chatting behind the closed door of the living room would give them enough privacy.

Sanna took the hint and went to pick up her handbag, which she had left in the hallway. She entered the living room and started to go through the papers. As Sarita emerged into the room with two mugs of coffee, Sanna gave copies of them to her.

Sarita eyed the papers with a haunted face, tears in her eyes. It was difficult for her to contemplate why she was the one taking care of everything. Martti would be able to do it so much better. Sanna explained to her calmly that due to Sarita being the nearest next of kin, taking care of matters was cast on her. Sanna affirmed this being the worst possible time to do this, but the sooner Sarita got the wheels rolling, the better. Sanna called Martti on behalf of Sarita and asked for a suitable lawyer to conduct the estate inventory. Martti promised to get in touch with one of his lawyer friends on the matter. That was a turning point, relieving Sarita's painful emotions, especially due to Sanna's promise to give her a lift to different official places. Sarita commended Sanna over and over again for her help, but Sanna shrugged it off by telling her how much help she had received in the same circumstances. They discussed Sanna's accident and its consequences for a while; it seemed to ease Sarita's sorrow, at least a bit.

Sanna wanted Sarita to understand how important it was for her to let herself grieve in the moments it felt overbearing; it would get easier in time. This wasn't the right time to verbalise it. In order to make Sarita feel better, Sanna proposed a lunch break. She was certain that Sarita was not making proper meals when she was alone.

Sanna found the fridge. Fortunately, there was a broad range of groceries, making it easy for Sanna to decide to make omelettes. During her lunch preparations, Sanna asked Sarita if Matias's moving in had been just an attempt to help a friend or if there were some other issues involved.

Sarita confessed that Mikael had never given any other reason. The previous spring, she had had a strange incident, making Mikael very anxious. Sarita had fainted at one of the faculty parties and Mikael had called an ambulance to take her into the emergency unit. She had no recollection of it, other than waking up in the hospital bed, strapped to an IV. They had told her about the overdose of some substance. She had no idea how it had ended up in her system. She hardly ever drunk more than a couple of ciders. She had almost forgotten all about it before Mikael's murder, but now it caught up with her. Matias had moved in soon after that. According to Mikael, Matias's breaking up with his boyfriend was the only reason. Sanna advised Sarita to tell the police everything; it could help them solve the case.

The food was ready quickly. Sanna asked Matias to join them because she wanted to combine forces with him in taking care of Sarita. Both youngsters started to gorge their omelettes as soon as they sat at the table. Having satisfied their hunger pangs, Sarita began questioning Sanna about Ex Tempore Ltd. Sanna replied willingly.

"Are you working here now or volunteering?" Sarita asked suddenly.

"I am working; Martti agreed to pay me during this period. I would have done it for free, though, due to you being in such a hard place with your sorrow."

"Thank you for the support. I am so lost doing this alone. Even my mother just keeps moaning but still not getting how I really feel. Now I could use some rest if you don't mind. Eating has made me feel better, but now I feel drowsy."

"I don't mind. I can leave now and pick you up on Monday at ten; we can start with the paperwork. When the solicitor calls, make an appointment and let me know. I can give you a lift. That way, we can check that one off of our list."

She put her coat on and, after saying goodbyes, took off to the parking space where she had left her car. Just as she was driving off, she spotted Juho and Antti's car beside the road. Antti's face was turned in her direction. Sanna waved her hand to him as she drove past. When Antti returned her salute, his puzzled face amused her.

Thank God I managed to get out in time! Sanna thought to herself whilst driving home. Juho might have lost his rag, seeing her sitting on Sarita's sofa. At this point, all they needed was to do their work in peace. She had no desire to distract them anymore. More importantly, Juho had already penetrated her ramparts, so letting him get even nearer scared her. That is, not before the murderer had been captured. Somewhere in the corners of her mind, she was certain that he would soon forget all about her existence.

"Did you notice who was driving that red Avensis?" Antti asked Juho, while walking towards Sarita's flat.

"Oh, the one that just passed us? Honestly, I didn't. Was it somebody we know?" Juho wondered at his workmate's amusement.

"Well, it just happened to be your pocket Venus."

"Are you suggesting that Sanna could have got here ahead of us, again?"

"You seem to have so many women after you that you cannot tell whose turn it is today," Antti teased Juho.

"That chase is just inside your head. All she wants to do is bitch about me."

"Sometimes, I do wonder how big an idiot a man can be as far as women are concerned. You are in the fast track to becoming a confirmed old bachelor, listening to classical music in the evenings and reading old masters. Should we be worried about you?"

"Ha, ha! You must have taken to heart Sanna's words about the wingman. I think we should concentrate on Sanna's businesses seriously. She seems to be a specialist in every sector by the look of it. Makes you wonder what kind of company this working girl is running, doesn't it? I mean, Topi insinuated her trafficking both drugs and girls."

Antti glanced at his partner with astonishment. He had never even considered Sanna having an alternative motive in helping Sarita. Maybe there was something in it. During their talks with the other members of staff, they had revealed Sanna had completed her degree in Helsinki. All the others had studied in Kuopio. Antti found this duality rather weird. He had always thought that the curriculum was the same, regardless of the location of the university. He suggested that Juho revise Sanna's student days; he was adamant she had something to hide. They might as well extend their investigations to all of the staff members as a sign of thorough scrutiny. Since Antti was pretty certain of

Sanna's innocence, despite Topi's words, he simultaneously proposed a bet on a boys' night out, including a Weasel's ice hockey game. Juho was also certain of his position and so they agreed on a two-week investigation time limit to ensure fair play on both sides.

Matias answered the door and led them to the kitchen. He told them Sarita was resting after her meal. He was still very distressed about his blackout, stating the same story he had told on Monday. Antti asked him about Sanna's visit. Matias had not heard their discussion due to them being in the living room, but he had the impression it concerned finances. They had mentioned getting a lawyer at some point, but he couldn't make a connection to what the real issue was.

Juho raised his eyebrows, as if saying: "I told you so!"

Antti shrugged his shoulders. There might be nothing in it. At the same time, they heard a phone ringing in Sarita's room. Sarita sounded matter-of-fact when she answered. It was easy to hear through the thin door that she was sorting out some kind of schedule. Juho moved nearer the door when he heard her speaking about Sanna and going to the bank the following week.

Sarita was still on the phone when she entered the room. She picked up a pen and made notes on some paper. After hanging up, she greeted the men with a smile.

"Martti's lawyer called and promised to meet me next week," she affirmed to Matias.

"What's the issue with the lawyer? Has somebody told you that you need a lawyer before talking to us?" Juho asked curiously.

Sarita seemed scared. Tears filled her eyes and her face

frowned: "Sanna didn't say anything of the sort. Do I need a lawyer for that as well? Sanna only said that I need a trustee for estate inventory."

Juho put his hands on Sarita's shoulders and assured her there was no added legal aid needed as they just wanted to have a chat with her. Juho walked her to the living room sofa. Antti observed the situation from the side. He had noted before how Juho's gentle manner had defused situations and this was the case even now. They didn't start Sarita's interview until she had calmed down.

"Is Sanna helping you out of the goodness of her heart or are you paying for her services?" Antti asked on behalf of them both.

"Martti and Sanna have made some kind of an arrangement – I don't pay her anything. She actually told me she wanted to help me for free after getting so much help herself in similar circumstances," Sarita explained, with a little annoyance.

"So, you know of Sanna's husband dying in an accident. Has Sanna told you anything else about it?" Juho enquired.

"Only that she went to bed in the evening as a wife and woke up a week later as a widow. Almost like me." Sarita wiped tears from her eyes.

"How well did you know Sanna before Mikael's murder?" Juho persisted.

"I met Sanna in the pharmacy for the first time when I had a panic attack, and Sanna made me breathe into the paper bag."

"And I met her as you came to wake me up with force, and I almost crapped myself," Matias joined in with Sarita.

"Did Mikael ever talk about work? Did he have any problems or strange occurrences there? Any gossip or funny stuff?"

Neither of them had any recollection of anything special. In the occasional shop talk, he sometimes referred to some amusing incidents, which they had difficulties in understanding. They had laughed at them and then forgotten them, since they seemed to be inside jokes only. Studying in Med School was so intense that they did not have the strength to pay attention to anything else.

Sarita played them Mikael's last voicemails from her mobile phone. Their time codes gave them a more accurate timeframe on his movements. Sarita was sad because she had only noticed in the morning that her phone's ringer was off, and she couldn't speak with her husband for the last time. Fortunately, the voicemails were still intact. She let the policemen listen to the messages. They copied them for more thorough scrutiny.

As the twosome drove from Linnanmaa back to Raksila, Juho pondered Sanna's conduct. On the outside she had courtesy, but underneath, there was always something sarcastic. Sanna was very generous when providing information, but at the same time, she seemed to leave bits and pieces out. Sanna seemed to feel at ease everywhere she went. At the same time, all the males around her agreed to pay whatever she happened to ask for her services.

He had started to have second thoughts about having so eagerly bet with Antti, but there was no way of backing out without losing face. Juho wondered why she was tantalising him so much. Juho had always liked independent and smart women. His former girlfriend, Lilja, popped up in his mind all of a sudden. She had ridden into his life like a Valkyrie and swept him off his feet once and for all. The relationship had been stormy. Lilja had had a hard time accepting Juho's career choice. In her opinion, Juho could have chosen something better than risking his life around the clock on such a low wage. They might have been able to work around their disagreements if Lilja hadn't suddenly announced she was leaving him and going to do research in Mayo clinic in the States, with the love of her life. Juho had at some level been relieved by her leaving, since their affair was dying slowly, anyway. After that, he hadn't met anyone so soul-stirring. Not before he met Sanna. This made his circumstances ambivalent due to Sanna making it clear what her thoughts of the twosome were.

However, the issues Topi had brought up must be investigated to the backbone, as they could reveal an appropriate motive. The drug squad had not supported his story of any new, big factors on the local drug scene. There was no connection between Sanna and Mikael. Sanna had clearly told the truth when she said that they had never worked at the same time at the Third. It was still possible that they met on some other occasion in their free time. There seemed to be all kinds of events on offer to the pharmacy staff. Mikael was sort of a staff member there and could have attended any of the activities the drug companies offered. Juho felt that the connection was too far-fetched due to their big age gap. They could have nothing in common apart from work. The forensic report indicated that there were a lot of files on knock-out drugs and date rapes on Mikael's computer; he was also interested in prescription forgeries, but none of his friends recalled ever discussing those topics with him. Those things had been covered in some lectures but not extensively. A few mentions in pharmacologic lectures in connection with drug abuse. Aleksi suggested the idea of him using it as a basis to his baccalaureate thesis. Fortunately, they had been in this situation many times before. The biggest issue for Juho was the missing motive.

He had gone around and around the case with Antti and constructed several possible chains of events. None of them seemed plausible. Juho had perused the boys' statements over and over again. It was no use at this point. Same thing happened with the interviews of the pharmacy staff members. Everyone had an appropriate alibi at the time of the events, including Sanna. And if Sanna wasn't a member of the regular staff, she was still one of them. That's why they wanted the killer to come from outside of their tight circle. He had never met a work community as grown together as this. Everybody seemed to know everybody else's business through and through, still keeping their personal and professional lives apart. Being a police officer, Juho had to keep an open mind to every possibility.

Since they had read the autopsy report all over again, it had occurred to both of them to contemplate the alternative theory that the fatal blows were struck by a woman, but Pasi had calculated the angles and the force needed. They were not compatible to any of the women in the pharmacy. Pasi had indicated that the striker must have been at least five foot nine; that fact cut all the females out of the picture.

TWELVE

ANTERO AND JUHO FOUND the next two weeks passed by really swiftly. They interviewed everybody involved several times over. Sanna was the only one avoiding a really good conversation. She answered when they called but agreeing a meeting turned out to be a challenge. Yet, Juho felt her presence in every discussion. Sanna's name was mentioned, though neither of the investigators made any reference to her. They had audited the annual reports of Ex Tempore with a fine-tooth comb as well as account information. Juho was getting more and more frustrated, until he received a phone call from a Helsinki drug squad detective, Olli Simanainen.

In the beginning, he introduced himself and enquired with scrutiny as to the motives of his colleagues' query. He was concerned if it had something to do with a big case they had several years ago, involving Sanna. Juho and Antti convinced him that they had a brand new one, after Sanna had found the body of her employer's son at their workplace.

Olli sounded relieved once he was convinced. He started off his own recollection. Their detecting had started at the university. A large quantity of weed had been circulated there. They had nicked a large number of sellers, but the identity of the big boss had been an enigma. They had their first coup when one of the sellers volunteered to be a snitch. He had freely given all the meeting places and times. They went slowly up the ladder of the organisation, but the top was still cloud-covered. Time and time again, the name Heikki Hänninen popped up, but this fellow had been able to cover his tracks. They had noticed that his girlfriend was a really foxy lady. After a while, she had vanished, or at least seemed to break up with Heikki. Finding out her identity and residence, they had decided to pay her a visit in order to interview her. They had had a specific preconceived idea about what kind of woman they were about to meet. To their surprise, the one answering the door was a sixteen-year-old-looking girl with braided hair, wearing a floral summer dress. Sanna had immediately verified their identity very carefully, before letting them in. She told them she had not expected any gentleman callers that day. She was very unsympathetic when they finally reached the point of asking about Heikki. Sanna declared that she'd thrown him out, after telling him that hell would freeze over twice before she was going to finance her fuck buddy's business dreams. She had no idea and couldn't care less where he resided. Just as the detectives were certain they had once again struck out, Sanna asked if they had tried the allotment cottage Heikki's parents owned in Marjaniemi. Sanna had heard him making arrangements to meet people there. As Heikki's perception of female intelligence was quite low, he never realised that Sanna had made the connection between him and Marjaniemi.

As a result, they had busted the whole gang, finding enough evidence in Marjaniemi for a conviction. They had managed to keep Sanna's name out, using a name found from Nabokov's popular novel, *Lolita*. Olli admitted them contemplating once in a while her present doings. Her quick wit had impressed them.

Juho replied that she still had it. Even the Gestapo interrogators would be envious of that. She seemed to be around every time something interesting was said. Olli admitted Juho being right and also smart enough to hear what she had to say. He sent his last regards to Sanna as well, before hanging up.

"Oh, well! Here we have quite a criminal mastermind. Shall we agree on me winning the bet and you treating me to a good games night, with the whole shebang?" Antti laughed at Juho's recollection of the call.

"That might cost me a fortune but let's put this case together before that. We can get to the Weasel game later on. Now, we have to have a good talk with Sanna. She is going to come clean this time. She seems to hear all the things nobody wants to share with us," Juho blustered.

"Aren't you dramatising a bit now? Stop that hanky-panky with Sanna immediately. For some reason, you have let her get under your skin. You have never before let women get between you and work."

"I have no hanky-panky with Sanna. She is the one running away every time we turn up. I have no idea how she does it, but it happens every time. As you know, I have called her several times, but she is always late from something. I think Sanna just has no desire to argue with me. It is hard to apologise to someone showing just her rear lights."

"Her rear lights are quite spectacular, aren't they?" Antti made fun of his pal.

"You do notice everything. I take it that you don't have enough work to do, since you have time to take interest in women's hind ends," Juho ragged back.

They started with a new will to go over the statements of the boys, trying to find inconsistencies, or at least something to sink their teeth into. Juho paid anew attention to Topi's claim about the night in Utopia, whereupon Mikael had shown Topi a female, resembling Sanna, involved in drug and girl trafficking. The tale dug into Juho's head, since there was no grounds to it. Anyway, Mikael had been worried about something. Sarita did tell them of her losing consciousness, causing Mikael concern for her safety. They had found Sarita's lab test results and they showed a high quantity of benzodiazepine in her bloodstream. Sarita had denied taking any medication that evening, meaning somebody else must have spiked her drink. That explained why Mikael had taken interest in the subject during his last months alive. Initially, there was no indication pointing at the culprit. The work was frustrating. There seemed to be nothing new they could find.

Finally, Juho threw the papers back on the table: "How come nobody has anything bad to say about Mikael? The boy must have been a saint. He did everything right, never even had a row with his wife. I can't get a grip on this guy at all on based on this data. He's never even got a speeding ticket in his life. As if he really never existed."

"Tell me about it! Nonetheless, this guy ended up with his head bashed in and nobody can figure out why. Have we checked his life insurance policy? I have no recollection of it in these papers," Antti reflected on his account.

"It has not been verified. His wife should know about it if there is one to be found. It should pop out initially in the estate inventory. Maybe we should get one of those lie detector gadgets Sanna claims to have installed in her head," Juho pondered half seriously.

"Yes, she alleged you talking a load of crap and then tried to pick you up."

"I suppose she wasn't totally wrong, although in my opinion, I was just trying to get her ladyship to understand not to toy with serious business."

"Maybe you should say it with more emotion. In my experience, women have a sixth sense on these things. My wife always points out when I talk through my hat. You are absolutely right. We should have a good talking to everyone involved and get a new perspective on the whole case."

They went over the questionnaire together and agreed on the order of the interviews. Everything was settled on a head start for the next morning.

THIRTEEN

AS SANNA MANAGED TO avoid meeting Juho and Antti, she got paranoid ideas about how thoroughly her life would be scrutinised.

Within days, she was thinking of the booze party the boys had. Mostly, she was interested in how quickly their inebriation had evolved. The other thing was the difficulty stealing the stuff. It was kept under lock and key at all times, as well as all the other chemical substances. Surgical spirit was used in many places, but nobody could drink it, since even a small dosage could kill you. In the past, rectified spirits were a basic booze choice for the medics and med students, but nowadays, it seldom moved over the counter in the pharmacy. She couldn't exclude the option they had taken some additional substances in order to get totally screwed. It would not be anything unexpected. It might not reveal the murderer, but it would tell them something about the motive. Nevertheless, Sanna was grateful to Martti for hiring her to help Sarita through this difficult time.

As the days went by, Sanna noticed how Sarita was moving forward in managing her sorrow. She had joined a grief group arranged by the parish with other grieving participants. Her loved ones and friends supported her as well. Step by step, Sarita had begun to distance herself from Sanna due to having sorted the official business in order. Sanna felt quite good about it. She understood how much stronger Sarita was than her outside appearance led people to believe. A part of the sorrow would follow her through life.

Once she had made sure Sarita was coping, she started to focus on her own situation. She had contacted her colleagues, especially Liisa at the Third. They had discussed Sanna returning back full-time several times over, but nothing specific had been decided.

Almost two weeks after Jaana and Anu's intervention, Sanna decided to call Jaana in order to chat about anything other than the ongoing murder investigation. During the phone call, Jaana suggested a little head reset evening between the three of them. It would be good to revise their endurance before the forthcoming pre-Christmas party season. Sanna could not resist the offer; a night together in female company might shine some light on the greyness of the autumn. Jaana promised to call Anu and if she agreed, she would text them both the meeting place. After hanging up, she headed straight to the shower.

They met at their usual place: The Ball of Rotuaari, and after a short negotiation, ended up in the upstairs restaurant Grill It! (the old fire station) to wine and dine.

Having finished their steaks, they went to the downstairs sports bar to have a chat. The bar was quite empty, but as often before, their chatting was interrupted by drink offerors. None of them had the guts to stay longer than one drink due to their way of cracking jokes. Fortunately, Sanna had no need to rely on her imaginary 'Japanese sumo wrestler boyfriend'. Suddenly, Sanna's attention focused on the male trio standing in the doorway. Since one of them was Matias, she deduced the other two were Topi and Aleksi. By the look of them, this wasn't their first watering hole of that evening, or they had spent another gaming night at somebody's flat. Sanna pointed the boys out to the girls and they set out to watch their next move. As the trio had managed to purchase their drinks, they stood for a while, searching of a free table. Finally, Matias's gaze stopped on Sanna. He said something to his friends, who turned their eyes in the same direction. Matias collected his courage and, once they agreed, sat at the ladies' table. After appropriate introductions, they began consulting Sanna on her finding Mikael's body and the conversation waved on through the boys' studies and on to her work as a pharmacist. They felt sorry because they had not looked after Mikael by helping him out with the cleaning that night. They had talked about it, but the boys insisted on it being just a joke. Sanna asked them if they were in the habit of helping each other with their work, but they denied it fiercely.

The night went on with light chatter. The boys made attempts to ask questions about Mikael. All of them knew of Sanna's part in the case. Therefore, they threw queries to her and dropped hints with the same allegedly relaxed attitude. The ladies contemplated everything they had heard on their visits to the ladies' room together. The drug aspect the boys were trying to establish especially amused them. The ladies had agreed to limit their alcohol consumption after the boys arrived at their table. It was easily arranged; gin and tonic looked the same without the gin. It proved to be a good idea due to Aleksi making passes at Sanna as the evening proceeded. The whole plot made Sanna feel awkward; after all, she was old enough to be the boy's mother.

Both Jaana and Anu had noticed Aleksi's strange behaviour and had pondered the reason for it on their visit at the ladies' room. They made a plan for their evening at the same time due to their blood alcohol level being over the limit. Sanna was especially eager to avoid an uneasy situation, arising from the fact that Aleksi might suggest taking her home. Anu phoned Alpo from the bar; he had promised to give them a lift home. On returning to the table, they made a show that their night was ending. The boys made a lame attempt to stop them going, with no effect on the women's desire to take off. When they were finishing their last drinks, Aleksi asked what kind of instrument was used to kill Mikael. Sanna denied knowing. Fortunately, Aleksi was satisfied with her answer and changed the subject. Although the ladies had already put their coats on, Aleksi went on trying and asked Sanna to join them to continue the night in Utopia club. Sanna declined the honour. The next day was a workday.

As they were walking across the yard out of the gate, Anu enquired as to what Aleksi had wanted. Sanna answered that she'd got an invitation to continue the night with them in Utopia. Anu and Jaana looked at each other. They both remembered Sanna's reaction on their one and only visit to the nightclub in question. The evening had started off very nicely. They had danced and had a few drinks, until all of a sudden, Sanna had become absent. When Sanna started panicking and speaking about ambulance lights, they had called it a night. Later on, Sanna had revealed having nightmares for at least a week afterwards. Sanna admitted how funny it must sound due to her not remembering the accident. In her dreams, there were only shapes and the lights of emergency vehicles. After that, Sanna took a fierce stand not to enter the premises ever again. It didn't stop Jaana and Anu teasing Sanna while they were waiting for Alpo to get there. In the end, they agreed to bet on Aleksi's capability to get her laid. Could he lure Sanna in to be his fuck buddy? They never even considered an alternative solution to his behaviour.

On the way home, they were too tired to try to get any more laughs out of it. Sanna thought that there must have been more behind it in connection with Mikael.

FOURTEEN

IN THE MORNING, SANNA was woken up by Liisa's call. She asked if Sanna would come to work in the pharmacy that day. Sanna had planned to take the day off in order to recover from the previous late night.

"We have been extremely busy since the local newspapers started writing headlines about this murder. We have all been busy bees since everybody needing medication seems to want it from us. And on top of that, all the monthly paperwork has to be dealt with," Liisa explained, stressed.

"Of course, I'll be there. Is it all right if I am a bit late?" Sanna asked, rubbing her eyes.

She pondered whether she was still over the limit, although she wasn't actually drunk any longer. Sanna got up from the bed, still speaking on the phone.

"Do you have a new cleaner or did Leila return early from her sick leave?" she asked on her way to the loo.

"I was fortunate to call your company. We got a really reliable temp here. Anu had someone called Annikki, who was more than happy to take the gig on such short notice.

Our technicians are so busy getting the reports done before the due date."

"Good for you! It is nice you were able to sort that out so quickly. See you soon." Sanna hung up.

Fortunately, she had an emergency stack of Berocca and Burana. She decided to get her morning coffee at work, grabbed a jar of curd and scooped its contents into her mouth hastily. Then, she got dressed. Instead of tying her hair back, she put on a headband to keep it out of her face.

"And now, put your chin on your chest and head towards new failures," she told herself as she took a quick peek at the end wall full-length mirror.

Even though Liisa had warned her, she was astonished at the large crowd when she arrived at Third. They had put a small table in the corner of the waiting area with Mikael's photo and an open guest book for people to leave their condolences in. Kristiina had told her that they had to put that table there in order to avoid people boxing the narrow pavement outside. The customers were eager enough to talk about Mikael or enquire about the details of the murder, anyway. The most sensitive ones were just embracing the atmosphere. Sanna, on the other hand, had no time or energy to listen to the buzz around her. When Sanna went down to get some lunch, she realised she hadn't brought any packed food with her. Fortunately, there was a lot of food brought by the clients and business collaborators.

She was having her lunch rotation with Kristiina again. She took advantage of their time together to catch up on recent events, ready to share mutually her own experiences of recent days. Kristiina grumbled how busy they had been. Occasionally, she felt they couldn't even take their statutory breaks. The apothecary had left Liisa in charge of the pharmacy, taking her out of customer service; administrational duties took her time up completely. As they were still sitting in the coffee room, Sanna told Kristiina about Mikael's friends and how they had bumped into them at a bar the previous night.

They exchanged a few words about Sarita, before Sanna asked her if Mikael had mentioned any issues that were of concern to him. Kristiina replied that she'd never heard him share anything of the sort with them. He had been very interested in processing the subscriptions in the pharmacy. Kristiina had always thought it was connected with the subscription doctrine course in his studies.

As they were finishing their break, Kristiina mentioned finding torn plastic bags in the tub containing outdated drugs, like someone was looking around for something. In her opinion, Kristiina should inform the police promptly about it, which she made a promise to do by the end of the day. Sanna started to collect her crockery and stack them into the dishwasher. She felt relieved that her slight hangover was evaporating. At closing time, everybody was able to let out a sigh of relief. It was Friday and they all had a free weekend ahead.

Monday was also a busy day. Nevertheless, Sanna had time to chat with her colleagues a bit more, since the haste had ceased from the previous week. Everyone was still in shock about Mikael's death. The police had talked to everybody several times over, but nobody had any inklings as to how Mikael had ended up in the spirits storage. Of course, all of them had their own ideas on the matter. Kristiina had, however, called Juho, who had promised to pay a visit to the pharmacy early this week with the forensic team. Sanna had her doubts that they would find anything. Nobody in their right mind would dig into it without wearing gloves.

The investigators didn't show up at the pharmacy until Wednesday. Sanna didn't even notice their arrival. She was busy enough checking the subscriptions and handing them out. She had no time to pay attention to her environment due to her work requiring her full concentration.

Just as she was checking out a big pile of subscriptions, she heard a male voice in the base of her ear: "Hey, Sanna, we should surely have a little chat? Or should I call you Lolita?"

Juho himself was startled by Sanna's reaction. Her face had gone pale and she looked like she was about to faint any minute. Sanna closed her eyes and leant on the counter, breathing heavily, until she managed to collect herself enough to control her voice trembling.

"I'll finish this off and then we can talk. Why don't you sit down over there until then," she said and pointed at a bar stool behind her.

Juho sat on the stool and stayed there, observing Sanna working.

Her hands were still shaking while sticking labels on the med bottles and marking the subscriptions on the table. She collected all the bottles and subscriptions into a plastic box after finishing her task. "Go and get your wingman so we can talk after I've given these out."

Juho stood up nicely and fetched Antti from the office, who was having a conversation with Liisa and Kristiina.

When they returned, Sanna was already waiting for them in the scale room doorway. They went inside together and Sanna closed the door behind them. Sanna turned to them, her face frowning, starting to grill them on trespassing into places without a permit. She ran her hands through her hair, causing her headband to fly onto the table while she was speaking. She grabbed it into her hands. She announced that they were as unreliable as Olli Simanainen, who had sworn secrecy on her part in their case. Probably, it was common knowledge in the police station by now and by the end of the day, it would be the talk of the town.

At this point of Sanna's speech, Antti assured her that they had only talked about it behind closed doors. No documents of it had been written. Olli had been very specific about everything before revealing anything. All they wanted was to arrange a meeting with Sanna. She could clear matters up. Sanna looked suspicious for a second but told them she would be at home after five if that time was convenient for them. Antti apologised on his behalf. It was his turn to collect his children from day care, since his wife had a late shift that night. Juho was relieved by the truce as he was already regretting his own words. He just wasn't able to resist the temptation of Sanna's reaction upon hearing him call her Lolita. If having realised beforehand Sanna's fear, he would never have mentioned it.

Before they let Sanna get on with her work, Antti asked, pretending to be casual, whether Sanna had ever visited Utopia. Sanna replied that she'd come to the conclusion that it wasn't a place for her, after going there around the time of it first opening a few years back. The flashing lights and the blasting music had caused her to have nightmares about police cars and ambulances for a period of time after her only visit there. She pondered their line of questioning. Antti had to explain that there was an eyewitness testimony of her being there at the same time as Mikael earlier in the autumn. Sanna burst into laughter and asked who had told them this cock and bull story. Hell would freeze over three times before she entered that facility ever again.

FIFTEEN

AS SOON AS SANNA got home, she started to make dinner. It would make talking to Juho easier, having something to naturally fill in the uneasy gaps of the conversation. It also gave her time to focus her thoughts on the discussion for the evening.

Juho proved to be prompt for his appointments. Sanna's doorbell rang exactly at 6pm. As Juho stepped in, Sanna realised that the smell of the food had reached him through the door. At first, Juho hesitated, but Sanna convinced him that it would be a pleasure to have somebody to share a meal with. He admitted that, being a bachelor, he didn't get many offers like that. He usually had lunch at work, and in the evenings, he favoured frozen dinners. They talked while eating, or rather it was Sanna doing the talking.

Sanna had moved to Oulu quite soon after her graduation from high school due to having received a study place from the Nursing School. Her big brother, Alpo, had moved here a couple of years prior. He had helped his little sister to obtain a dormitory room in a shared flat with two mates in Välkkylä.

It was the same dormitory where Alpo shared a condo with Pasi and Sami. Sanna resided with Jaana and Anu, both single at that time. It all changed after Alpo took his mates to their housewarming party, where they all hooked up with each other. The girls had the idea of Ex Tempore after having a few bottles of wine. After a little while, they had got fed up with having to go back and forth between two flats, so they rented a detached house in Rajakylä. It remained their place of residence until they had all graduated. Sanna had ended up in the Central Operation Department, Sami in the ER. Pasi had often been in the same theatre with Sanna, evolving their friendship into a good working relationship. Around a year after Sanna and Sami had purchased this flat, they had agreed to apply to study in Helsinki. Sanna decided to get a degree in pharmacology and Sami had received a study place in the Health Technology Department. They spent a gap year before their studies working as nurses in London. Moving to Helsinki into a small studio flat in Roihuvuori had been easy with the help of their friends. After the first semester, they had just intended to spend their Christmas holiday in Oulu, visiting relatives. That journey ended in the fatal accident, making Sanna a widow and Sami an organ donor. Sanna had also lost a whole week of her life. Her first memory of the hospital was meeting Juho. For some reason, Sanna had imagined him coming to her bedroom at home. Afterwards, her friends hadn't believed her claims of a policeman visiting her. In the end, even Sanna had been convinced of the fact and they had started to refer to Juho as her 'dream man'. Sanna's mother had moved in to help her daughter. After a lengthy rehabilitation, she had returned to

Helsinki to get on with her studies. The first year, all she did was to go to the lectures and then return to her flat. It was a pure survival game for Sanna.

It lasted until Jaana and Anu decided to take a tight grip on her life by coming to Helsinki a couple of weeks before the academic year ended. Intervention had been a success beyond all expectations. Sanna's final healing had begun after that. Her last study year had been easier; she had taken on the indulgence of the capital with enthusiasm. Heikki had come into her life from one of the faculty parties that same autumn. Their affair had been short but intense over the winter. It had ended when Sanna had made it clear that she would not finance his businesses. The killing blow had been a visit from a nark to Sanna's flat at the end of the spring. After that, Sanna had realised her vulnerability and returned back to Oulu. She had taken the rest of her courses remotely.

The return had proved to be more complicated than she had anticipated. The whole world had moved on and nothing had remained the same. The hardest thing for her was being the only single one in her circle of friends. After Heikki, she had been more than happy about that fact, but then Janne had come along, with a nice feeling of having a future together. The long relationship had come to an end when Janne had got an offer to build a hospital in Tanzania. He had left towards new challenges with joy, leaving no strings attached at home.

That was when Sanna noticed that she also had to make changes in her life. This autumn, she had finalised her plan just before Mikael was murdered. Finding Mikael's body and everything connected to it had brought up old things, throwing her off balance. It reminded her of her starting point, i.e turning over a new leaf in her life.

Sanna held her tongue momentarily, cocked her head to one side, gazing at Juho: "Did that answer your question, although it was a little bit delayed?"

Juho frowned his brows: "Yeah, I guess. As if I knew what the original question was."

"You asked me in the hospital whether I remembered what had happened. Since then, you have emerged in my dreams once a year, asking the same. I have always woken up before I could give you an answer."

"Did that amnesia really take the whole week away?"

"Yes, it did. It was like a black hole had sucked me in. That was why it was so easy for me to believe you were just a dream. It was not like remembering eating sausage and chips or drinking refined spirits. Those were the two things Matias could remember of the lads' night out the very next day."

"That's news to me. None of the boys mentioned eating sausage and chips in their statements. That is something we should have a closer look at. After all, the same stodge was found in Mikael's stomach in the autopsy."

"It took me a while to make the connection. It made perfect sense that they had something to eat before boozing. It might just be a shot in the dark, but it would make it easier to establish the time of death. The other issue is the stolen spiritus fortis. Did you find out where or who had taken it? It is very well-guarded stuff, isn't it?"

"We haven't thought about checking either of them. We have been so busy taking statements," Juho fretted, his memory lapsing inwardly.

He continued on the evening's topic: "Let's get back to your amnesia. Have you ever made an effort to regain your recollection?"

"I was given a chance to discuss it with a psychiatrist during my rehab. He suggested hypnosis but I declined it. In my opinion, my brain had buried all of it deep down for a reason; I didn't want to poke it any more than that."

"I know exactly what you mean. We all have things that are better forgotten."

"You must be the first person really getting my feelings on it. Most people think I have a desire to get a *Bold and Beautiful* type of scenario, where Sami comes back through the door and I live happily ever after with him, as if the accident never took place. In reality, I haven't even dreamt of him ever since."

Sanna was referring to former in-laws, who had made it clear to her that she should hold a torch to Sami's memory and never ever remarry. It all began when Sanna had acted according to Sami's living will, giving her consent on the organ donation. The next thing was her mother-in-law's taking on the funeral arrangements. In her opinion, Sanna was not an appropriate person to take care of such a demanding operation. At that point, Sanna's mother, Terttu Taipale, had taken her daughter's side on the matter. The bitter war had gone on over Sanna's hospital bed until she had drawn a red line on the matter. She had made it clear to her mother-in-law, Saimi, how things were going to be arranged. The funeral would be held in Oulu and after that, the lady could bury her son wherever she wanted. If that was something she couldn't agree with, Sanna would have her husband cremated and scatter his ashes in the sea. Saimi had complied reluctantly. And took her daughter-in-law off her Christmas card list at the same time. Pasi had told Sanna that Saimi had invited his parents to Sami's birthday parties and the memorial of his dying day, since they still resided as next-door neighbours in Taivalkoski. Sanna had never got an invitation to either of them. It suited Sanna perfectly.

The food had done its job. Juho must have been starving as there was nothing left.

"It just occurred to me how much you remind me of the British TV chef Nigella Lawson. You could be sisters."

"So, you watch cooking shows? It seems a strange hobby for a policeman."

"I am not that hooked on them. As it happened, I just turned on the channel she was on and I stuck around watching her cook. There was something so sensual about it that I had to watch the whole show end-to-end. It doesn't matter whether you are in the pharmacy or autopsy, you have a similar flair in you."

"Thanks for the compliment! You must have had a really intimate moment with Nigella."

Juho looked at Sanna, pondering if he should get angry with her. Then, he noticed a glimmer in Sanna's eyes. He laughed: "Nice try! A gentleman doesn't kiss and tell that easily."

"Now that we're opening up, I can tell you how much you remind me of Danny Messer. Your hair is particularly Danny Messer style."

"Do you mean that CSI New York guy? Nobody else has ever noticed it."

"Maybe your own style is so strong that nobody realises it. Antti, on the other hand, is more like the actor Taisto Reimaluoto."

"How true that is!"

Sanna put the coffee maker on and suggested a short toilet break before they continued their discussion further. Juho said it suited him well. Sanna could go first due to her greater need for a break. Sanna replied that there were two toilets in the flat: one in the powder room and one in the bathroom.

Sitting on the toilet seat, Sanna realised she was stretched tighter than a drum. She struggled to relax before she could empty her bladder. Tears started to pour from her eyes uncontrollably. She leant her elbows on her knees, covering her face with her hands. She heard Juho finishing in the bathroom and moving around the flat. Sanna tried instinctively to keep as quiet as she could so that he wouldn't hear her crying. It would be very difficult to explain the feelings completely taking over her. Recollecting memories had brought everything to the surface. This was the first time for a long time she had discussed it. Today, the circle would close. In between her crying, she felt relief. The past was truly behind her and she could be free and whole again. At the same time, she listened to the sounds coming from the flat. Everything was quiet. Maybe Juho had got fed up with waiting and left the building.

While Sanna was still in the powder room, Juho took some time to look around. He had noticed two closed doors leading out of the living room. First, he opened the door on the right, finding a bedroom being used as a home office. A desktop computer was on the table under the window, with a printer to the side. On the wall across from the window stood a high Lundia bookcase full of books. Juho leaned forwards to study the backs of the books. The bottom shelf was full of thick volumes of professional reference books. Other shelves were entirely different matter. Apparently, Sanna's interests leant towards detective stories. Juho thought how amused Antti would be, making sharp comments about her reading habits. Antti had a tendency to secretly study people's bookcases and share his conclusions on car journeys. Usually, he hit the nail on the head. The diversity of Sanna's bookcase would have been a real treasure to Antti. On the shelves, there was Mma Ramotswe, Modesty Blaise and Jane Marple in good harmony. Beside them were many others Juho had never even heard of.

While browsing the contents of the bookcase, Juho listened to the noises coming from the powder room. Or the lack of them. He straightened his back and left the room, closing the door behind him. Juho sneaked into Sanna's bedroom. Its decor was feminine and cosy. A large bed with a white, metal rung headboard occupied the middle floor space. The bedspread was decorated with brownish geometrical patterns and the curtains doubled the colour scheme. On the door side corner of the room stood a white painted dressing table with a mirror on its raised cover. On the other side of the table was a small, tree-shaped jewellery rack. Juho had seen similar items in the jewellery departments of supermarkets but had never quite figured out their purpose. Finally, he got it. On the branches of the tree, she had hung up bracelets, necklaces, rings and earrings. He had just leant over to get a better look at Sanna's jewellery selection when he noticed her standing behind him.

"Do you want to play dress-up games with me?"

"I have never before realised what these things are used for," Juho replied, straightening his back.

Sanna had taken off her pink cardigan in the powder room and dangled it in her hand. She threw it on the headboard before leaving the room. After putting the coffee cups on the living room table, she asked if Juho would dare to drink a glass of wine before he drove home. Without waiting for his answer, Sanna poured the wine into two glasses. Juho sat on the sofa. Sanna sat on an armchair which was cornerwise to the sofa. She pulled her feet under her. They lifted their glasses before the first sip. Juho saw that Sanna had removed her make-up.

Juho asked, after a momentary consideration, if he had done or said something to upset Sanna, since her stay in the powder room had taken so long. Sanna replied that it was not his fault. The tension building up for weeks had just burst out. Reminiscing about the past had surfaced her emotions and now, everything was better than ever.

Sanna changed the subject almost on the fly. She clearly didn't want to talk about her moment of weakness. Sanna and the girls' meeting with the boys in the bar got Juho to focus on the matter of business. As their chatting went on, Juho got the idea that Sanna had left something out. He was right about that. Sanna hadn't mentioned Aleksi's flirtation at all. It was irrelevant to the whole story. Or that was something she wanted to believe.

"How did you girls make them reveal all of this just like that?" Juho pondered.

"After all, we were all a teenage boys' wet daydream in

that situation. Three hot, drunken nurses marvelling at the great intelligence of med students. In their dreams, all nurses are wannabe doctors, if they just had brains."

"Would the situation be different if Antti and I were women?"

"Of course, it wouldn't. In those teen boys' eyes, you are the manly men. Nurses, on the other hand, are the motherly figures putting their cool hand on the patient's forehead. And if your story is touching enough, you can rest your head on her motherly bosom. The rest you can find in every porn film ever made."

"So, if asked what's the difference between a policeman and a normal man, that would be your answer?"

"The policeman comes when invited. A normal man comes when he wants," Sanna stated, holding a straight face, with laughter in her eyes.

Sanna could judge Juho had understood her true meaning without further explanations, hearing him laugh.

He looked at his watch secretly and was astonished how long he had stayed. Juho decided not to prolong his visit. It didn't feel right by Sanna. Juho himself was used to long interrogations, but he got the feeling that Sanna would have trouble continuing much longer. He emptied his glass accordingly, before he got up from the sofa: "Thank you for the good meal and wine! It was good to talk things over properly. We'll have to do this again sometime."

"Well, I'm glad you enjoyed it."

As Sanna got up from her chair, she stumbled precariously. Without thinking, Juho grabbed her hand, put his other arm around her waist and pulled her into his arms.

Sanna stood still for a second and leant against his chest. They stood there, for what felt like forever, until Sanna lifted her head and looked Juho in the eyes.

"I take it this doesn't make any sense at all," she said.

"With you, nothing makes any sense whatsoever. It's better if I leave now so you, too, can get your beauty sleep," Juho sighed.

"Sleeping is overrated. Anyway, I cannot sleep at all without my cuddly toy. Do you know any volunteers for the job?" Sanna was amused by her own boldness.

The movements of her body sent thousands of lightning bolts to his nerve endings. He pressed his face down on Sanna's hair and murmured quietly.

"Maybe I can volunteer for this position if it is still available. I don't just work all the time. Even Joe Cool needs to idle sometimes," Juho teased.

Sanna pushed him a little further back and looked straight into his eyes.

"Are you being serious right now?"

He replied by pressing his lips to Sanna's mouth. At the same time, he took a few steps backwards, until he felt the edge of the sofa behind his knees. He sat on the sofa and pulled her legs onto his lap and withdrew himself a little further. Sanna laughed as she sat straddling his lap. She took Juho's hands and wrapped them around her waist. She crossed her fingers behind his neck. They started kissing passionately and Juho's hands began exploring the insides of her shirt.

SIXTEEN

JUHO WAS LYING IN Sanna's bed, holding her under his arm, her head leaning on his shoulder. Her face was pressed against his chest. Sanna was breathing slowly in and out, sniffing his skin. Sanna had lifted her other leg on top of him. Her knee was bent so it rested on his lower body. Sanna's hand played lightly with his chest hair. Her touch felt soft, like a butterfly wing. All of a sudden, he saw that life without Sanna was not an option anymore. He wanted to share his future with this woman. It was a surprising thought; nobody else had ever made him contemplate it. The sensation was so thrilling that he wanted to share it with her right away.

Sanna obviously could sense him willing to say something, since she moved her hand to his mouth and pressed it shut with her forefinger. Juho saw laughter glimmering in her eyes in the faint light coming through the window. As Sanna realised he was getting the message, she started caressing his face with her hand.

Juho lifted his other hand and started to move it down to her thigh, towards the knee. He felt a scar on top of it.

He began rubbing it with a similar stroke as he had seen Sanna do. At the same time, he could hear her breathing getting heavier and her body pressing harder against him. He bent to kiss Sanna as he let his hand slide down onto her shin. He felt the same scar pattern going down. Suddenly, he remembered Pasi's words about an overnight operation saving her legs. For some reason, the pure thought of it made him want her even more. He spun on the bed, positioning himself on top of Sanna. He held her by her ankles and let his hands slide across her body until they reached Sanna's breasts. She moved her body, trying to get as near him as possible. When Juho pushed himself inside Sanna, her hands pressed him against her. They found the same beat quickly and climbed all the way to the top together.

In the morning, Juho woke up alone in the big bed. He wanted to lie down a bit and enjoy the memories of the night. He had woken earlier, at dawn, finding Sanna on top of him. They had made love half asleep. Afterwards, Juho had fallen back to sleep, with the sound of Sanna's steps drifting away was his last recollection of that moment in the wee hours.

A smell of frying bacon and eggs, mixed with a strong coffee aroma, hovered in the open bedroom door. Juho jumped out of the bed and only then realised his nakedness. Fortunately, Sanna had hung his boxers and T-shirt on the headboard. He got dressed and headed towards the powder room when Sanna, in her short-legged pyjamas, noticed him. She turned her head while turning the eggs in the frying pan.

"Good morning, Sleepyhead! There is a toothbrush ready for you on the side of the sink."

Juho nodded and carried on. After completing his tasks,

he opened the mirror cabinet of the toilet in order to find something to shave with. Once nothing was to be found, he returned to the kitchen. Sanna was standing there in the angle formed by countertops, her back turned, waiting for the coffee to drip.

Juho walked behind her and put his arms around her. He slid his hands under her shirt and caressed her breasts for a moment. He kissed Sanna's neck and said: "You are quite a sly fox, Milady."

Sanna leant against him before answering: "Is it because I happen to like eating and shagging?"

Juho started to laugh and pulled away.

"Well, that too. You lure everybody into doing whatever you want. You made us run around in circles trying to catch our tails. You could have told us everything at the beginning but chose the other way."

"After all, what fun would that be? I just wanted to cover my arse. The world is a bad place for a lonely woman. I cannot make people do what I want – I encourage them to do what they want to do, anyway."

Juho sat on the table, where a steaming breakfast waited for him. Sanna placed the full coffee mugs in front of them. They started eating in silence. Juho lifted his eyes once in a while as he was eating to enjoy the chance of watching her in peace.

Sanna returned his gaze with a challenge: "Are you having second thoughts about last night?"

"And why on earth would I do that? I was precisely where I wanted to be. I couldn't have left you after you'd been crying. It was my fault in the first place, wasn't it?"

"So, you did it just from the goodness of your heart. I never thought I would end up being a charity case this early in my life. I hope you got a little pleasure for yourself as well."

Sanna's blast caught Juho off-guard totally. He got up, grabbed Sanna's waist and pulled her onto his lap. Then, he pressed Sanna's hand on his bulging fly front.

"As you probably noticed, there is nothing charitable going on. All I want to do now is to stay put and be cuddly with you. Unfortunately, I must go to work and do what a man's gotta do." Juho tried to look sad due to their incoming parting.

Sanna rubbed Juho's cheek tenderly: "You'd better shave that stubble off before you leave. You'll begin to resemble Rudolf the Robber otherwise. You can find razor blades and shaving foam in the bathroom cabinet."

"What are you doing today? Are you going to work? I can drive through town."

"Pretty normal day at the office. A mere giving out and putting in from dawn till dusk. And you will be busy enough picking up and putting down."

"You can express it the way you want."

As Juho finished his morning routine, Sanna had already got dressed. She was sitting at her dressing table, applying make-up.

"Is there something still bothering you?"

"The only thing is that I have no idea who you really are. You just come and go. If you told me that you live in a tent in Nallikari, I'd have no choice but to believe you."

Juho pondered a little while.

"And that's why you didn't let me speak last night?"

"What's your point? We weren't there to make speeches."

"I thought you were like a butterfly: difficult to catch however fast one tries to run after you. I was wondering why you kept sniffing me so closely?"

"I had to make sure that you were real and not just a dream," Sanna smiled happily.

She had finished with her face while they were talking.

"If your offer of a lift is still on, I would love to come to town with you."

Once they got to town, they agreed that Juho would call her in the evening just to make sure she was okay. Privately, he just wanted to hear her voice. It would be enough for the time being. As they were separating, they shared a long kiss goodbye.

SEVENTEEN

AT THE WORKPLACE, ANTTI was anxiously waiting for the results of his colleague's interview.

"The boss wanted a little briefing from us today. He wasn't that pleased with our progress on this case. Did you find out anything new yesterday?" he pried.

"Well, we talked a lot about everything. Let's go to the meeting room so we can all compare our notes together," Juho answered.

They found their boss already inspecting the board as they entered.

"Good thing you came in. Now, I want a good heads-up on your investigation. Ville and Antero will be here in a jiffy."

When the team was gathered together, Juho went over the results to get everyone up to date. They hadn't found a financial motive, not even a life insurance policy. The forensic team's visit to the pharmacy proved to be a waste of time. After that, he moved on to walk them through the new data Sanna had revealed to him. It was a short version of her tale of the bar evening spent with the boys. They contemplated the details, comparing them to the statements the trio had given. Trying to find inconsistencies in their stories was one of their goals in order to break their alibis. In the end, they settled upon pondering Sanna's mention of the sausage and chips, which none of the boys had remembered to refer to. The autopsy report indicated that Mikael's stomach contents consisted of beer, sausage, chips, onions and cucumber salad. According to digestion, the food had been taken in a couple of hours before death. Juho got on with drawing a timeline of final sightings of his movements. He had departed his friends around 4pm. Security cam video between 5 and 6pm. Alarm set at 6.30pm.

Juho continued the meeting by mentioning Topi's disclosure of one of the pharmacy staff members being involved in drug and girl trafficking, using Utopia as her base. He had claimed Mikael had shown him a female resembling Sanna as the head of the whole organisation. Sanna herself had denied that. The drug squad had no confirmation of the activity, but they had promised to look at it more thoroughly after hearing his statement. So far, they hadn't been able to confirm his claims one way or another. The paperwork from Ex Tempore showed no discrepancies. Antti seemed to contemplate something while the others were going through Ex Tempore's business. As the others were finishing beating around the bush, he opened his mouth and asked whether anyone had taken photos of the wedding and high school graduation pictures on display in the coffee room at the Third. They rummaged through the crime scene photos but none of them were to be found. Antti explained that he wanted to see if there was anyone resembling Sanna.

Antti phoned Liisa, requesting her to send the missing photos in digital form with the names attached. Fortunately, Liisa didn't question his request but promised to deliver them promptly to Antti's email address. She was a woman of her word as the photos were in Antti's inbox in a quarter of an hour. They gathered around the monitor together to go over them. It took some time to find the right one among the wedding pictures. They all sighed with relief. The bride was a curvy brunette, in her wedding gown anyway. It was obvious that the photo was taken a few years prior due to her being in her early twenties. That's where the joy ended. A speedy phone call revealed that she was heavily pregnant and had never visited the nightclub in question. The local Association of Peace was a more likely place for her. It made the men reconsider the truthfulness of Topi's whole statement.

After the meeting, Juho and Antti returned back to their common office to start going over the logs of their interrogation, based on their new information. Once they had sat on their bureaus, Antti made sure that the door was tightly shut. Then, he looked at Juho strictly and said: "I gather you didn't go home last night?"

"And how can you tell?" Juho replied with annoyance.

"Well, you don't need to be a rocket scientist to see it. You had the same T-shirt on yesterday. And since you don't seem to have a hangover at any rate, I concluded you have spent the night in a certain Sihtikuja condo," Antti stated. "Can we now deduce from that that the bachelor has given his last rose and is now off the market?" He continued his mocking.

"Isn't there a saying that one swallow doesn't make the summer?" Juho replied evasively.

"And neither does one fuck make a relationship, as it seems you are so under the weather," Antti nagged in earnest to Juho.

"Everything is okay between us. We agreed that I'll call her tonight. I hope she will stay under the radar, at least over the weekend," Juho clarified his foul mood.

"Do you have any concrete information that she's in danger or is it just something relating to your past experience?"

"Probably, there is the little voice of experience whispering in my ear. Especially when you remember what happened to her in Helsinki. She said that the guy was good company, until she realised that he was some sort of wannabe philanderer. Sanna herself wanted to forget all about it, but then we dug it up. It's for the best that we drill as deep into the action when it comes to the boys."

Antti burst into laughter, hearing Juho's story.

"Where did those sausage and chips emerge into the picture? Matias mentioned only being around the town."

Juho drew out from among the papers the autopsy report Pasi had given him and opened it on the page where the stomach contents were analysed. Matias had mentioned it to Sanna. For some reason, it wasn't in Matias's statement. They took out the Google maps page. They used it to seek the most direct way from Hallituskatu to the Third Pharmacy. There were no other grill kiosks on the way other than Piccolo Grilli in Letku Park and Kino Grilli, within a stone's throw of the Third. After pondering it for a moment, they asked Antero and Ville to go to both of them to enquire if some of the boys had purchased their stodge from either of them. They both agreed that it was a question of them grasping at straws. That might be the lever they needed to break their alibi.

EIGHTEEN

WHILE VILLE AND ANTERO were carrying out their task, they decided to phone Jaana and Anu to verify Sanna's tale of their evening out at the bar the previous week. They might also have some new information that Sanna had forgotten to mention.

Antti decided to call Jaana first to make an appointment with her. After a few rings, the call went to voicemail, so he left a message. As it happened, Anu was available and insisted on them meeting at Street Cafe for lunch. She was free for an hour, around midday. Later on, she had a long day ahead. She justified her request by pointing out that even policemen had to eat in order to restore their strength during a busy workday.

Prior to the call, Juho suggested to Antti that they could watch the security video where Mikael was cleaning up the pharmacy customer area once more. In Juho's opinion, the lad on the video could just as well have been Topi or Matias in a foggy video. Juho reasoned his thought on the timeline Pasi had given between his meal and death. In other words, what if Mikael had been lying on the spirits store floor already dead, while his murderer was finalising his own alibi. Antti went along with his partner's idea. Unfortunately, the quality of the security video was so blurry that it was really difficult to tell any facial details. They decided to drop the CD off to the lab on their way to town, hoping they could enhance the disk so the facial recognition could be ensured.

Due to getting the matter of the video underway, they began to make inquiries about the theft of the refined spirits. Since they had emphasised it had happened in the Med Lab, Antti called the university info number straight away, where he was connected to the person in charge of the inventory control of laboratories. Antti was surprised when he found out that the person he was trying to get in touch with worked in the Oulu University Hospital dispensary.

They began to work diligently, but as the clock was nearing midday, they were more than glad to have a concrete reason to take a break on their ineffective inquiries.

As they emerged at Street Cafe, they both ordered the Salad of The Day. Having managed to collect their portions, they stood a moment to look for Anu. At last, Antti's gaze hit a female in her mid-thirties, wearing a business-like trouser suit and a pink T-shirt. She had pulled her blonde hair up with a big hairgrip called a shark tooth.

She waved at them invitingly, in a semi-standing position. Once they arrived at the table, Anu reached out her hand, first to Juho: "Anu Taipale. You can call me Anu. It is so nice to finally meet Sanna's 'dream man'." She smiled at Juho mischievously.

Then she turned to Antti and said: "And you must be Antti."

Juho looked at her, astonished: "How on earth could you tell who is who? We've never met before. Did Sanna describe us to you?"

"No, it was Jaana Lampinen. You met her at Lilja's Doctorate dinner a few years ago," Anu replied.

Juho instinctively thought that she'd left out some information and got himself thinking about what had happened there to make Jaana remember him particularly. He recalled being introduced to Pasi's wife, but he wouldn't recognise her after so many years.

"Since you haven't come here just to reminisce, you must have some real issues concerning me. I have tried to think of what that could possibly be."

"We want to ask you about that recent evening out with you, Jaana and Sanna. Was it last Thursday?"

"Yes, we were having a girls' night out. When did Sanna tell you about that?" Anu pondered.

None of them noticed a youngster sitting at the table next to them, straightening up suddenly. He dug his smartphone from the side pocket of his backpack and keyed into it for a short time. Then, he lifted the backpack onto the table and put the phone back in the side pocket, as near to the next table as he could get it. At the same time, he tried to make sure that the people at the next table wouldn't recognise him. He pretended to be concentrated on the Evening News in front of him. The beginning of the conversation was not the least bit interesting but the mention of Thursday evening was his wake-up call. Especially since the female talking to the policemen turned out to be the one spending the evening at the sports bar the previous week.

"I went to see her last night and it came up in our conversation," Juho replied to her.

"As in, you two didn't go together?" Anu specified.

"No, we didn't because I had something else I needed to attend to. We thought there would be no harm in having a tête-à-tête about things," Antti cleared the situation.

"Did you get a proper breakfast before you left for work in the morning?" Anu asked.

Looking astonished, Juho answered her: "It tasted really good. Thanks for asking. You seem to have a full report on last night."

"I haven't talked with her since the weekend. I thought you two had a lot of catching up to do. It can easily take hours on end."

Juho looked at Anu, contemplating. Then he went back to their original reason i.e. the events taking place on their boozing night.

Anu remembered the events the same way Sanna described. She told them Aleksi's advances. On top of everything, Aleksi had made attempts to get Sanna to join them in Utopia. It came as a total surprise to Juho; Sanna hadn't mentioned the fact at all. Anu said that they realised that it had been a typical shagging bet between the students. At the end of the discussion, Antti asked about the sausage and chips. Anu's reply to the question was simple. They'd had a good meal beforehand and none of them had had any desire to stand in the queue in front of Kino Grilli in the middle of the night. Finally, Anu glanced at her watch and told them that she had to get back to the grind. She wished Juho and Antti a good day and sent her regards to Sanna. After shaking hands with the men, she walked away, clattering her high heels out of the cafe.

The youngster on the next table exited just after her. He headed towards the Third Pharmacy. The turn of the discussion had awakened his curiosity.

Juho and Antti stayed to get their free coffees. When they returned to the table, Antti blurted out: "Well, well, Sanna's honest-to-god 'dream man'! To what do we owe that honour?"

"I did tell you about my visiting Sanna at the hospital after the collision. Apparently, no one else saw me or believed Sanna when she told them about it."

"And Mrs Lampinen remembers you from the Doctorate dinner of your former partner. It must have been a hell of a party."

"I was introduced to so many people that I have no recollection of what Pasi's better half looked like."

They finished their coffees in silence. Both deep in their thoughts. As they left to head back to their workplace, they concentrated fully on their work.

Just before Juho and Antti decided to leave the rest of the checking to the next day, Antti asked whether Juho had made plans to secure Sanna's safety. Juho said he had promised to phone her that night. Antti's opinion was that Juho should invite Sanna to spend the weekend with him. She could at least be safe until they could nick the perpetrator. Juho agreed that it was a good idea. A weekend without any distractions could do them both good. Nobody would have any idea to look for Sanna at his place.

He phoned Sanna only around 7.30pm, since he wanted to give her time to get settled after the workday. It took only a couple of rings before she answered.

"Good evening, Charmer. How has your day been?" Sanna's relaxed voice was heard through the phone.

"We had a really eye-opening chat with your friend Anu today. You didn't tell me everything about that bar evening, did you?" Juho began laughing.

"Is that so? Maybe I forgot something. Do you think it was relevant?" There was reservation in Sanna's voice.

"Come on! You were invited to an after-party with the boys. Did you truly think it wasn't important?"

"If you put it that way, then yes. I thought that it was more of an inside joke between the lads. They wanted to test how pleased I was, getting the attention of future doctors. Having been a little bit more sober, and a little younger, I might have taken a chance to see how long it took before they cracked," Sanna reconciled.

"That is one way of putting it." Sanna's frankness made Juho laugh. "Would I get the same answer if I asked you to spend the oncoming weekend at my place?" Juho went on, bantering.

Sanna burst out with laughter: "You'll find out just by asking."

"I do have to be at work on Saturday. I could pick you up after that." Juho noticed himself sounding a bit too pleading.

"How do you think a weak woman can resist such a sincere request?" Sanna let out another coo of laughter way down her throat.

"Can you estimate how long it will take on Saturday?"

"I'll call you tomorrow; I might have a better picture then. Good night; sleep tight." Juho made a kissing sound down the phone.

"And you too!" Sanna kissed back.

NINETEEN

IN THE MORNING, JUHO began his round of calls to all those places where they had made inquiries. There wasn't a single bottle of refined spirits missing from the OUH. Juho wasn't the least bit surprised. After all, Sanna had also thought the boy's tale was a little wonky. Juho had a gnawing feeling that Sanna had said something essential regarding her amnesia. He decided to let it boil in the back of his mind, knowing it would pop up, as it had done on so many occasions in the past.

Antti had spent his morning down at the forensic lab to find out if the security cam picture was able to be enhanced so they could make a positive ID of the cleaner being Mikael. When he finally returned with the enlarged photos, they were able to recognise Mikael's face. It didn't exclude the possibility of him having a helper with him. Somebody must have been there in order to put the alarm on after Mikael's death. They haven't been able to prove that any of the boys ever visited the crime scene. Matias was the only one who ever admitted to being in the pharmacy as a lad with Mikael. Anyway, they had spent a lot of time at each other's homes, since Matias was Mikael's childhood friend.

All of a sudden, Juho got the idea to ask Liisa to confirm the fact. It was a true possibility that others had been there or met Mikael at work at some point. Liisa remembered the apothecary arranging a tour around the pharmacy for Mikael's tutoring group at the beginning of their orientation studies. The apothecary had personally taken them round the facility. Having done some digging, she read the list of the participants to Juho on the phone. Juho was once again pleased with her professional approach to all his inquiries. She never wondered or hesitated to answer any of their questions. It made Juho wish everybody else shared her clarity.

Jaana couldn't make an appointment with them on Thursday, but they had agreed to meet mid-morning on Friday.

Jaana arrived punctually. As she saw Juho, she smiled: "You haven't changed a bit since we last met!"

Juho smiled back at her, while trying to form an appropriate answer to her comment. He looked at Jaana with an appraising gaze, hoping to find even something familiar.

Her short, carrot-coloured hair was combed straight back with gel. Her looks and feisty attitude reminded him of Drew Barrymore. Black leather jacket, jeans and black boots made the resemblance even bigger. On her shoulder was a multicoloured backpack. There was amusement in her eyes: "You seem not to remember me from the after-party. It is no wonder. Back then, I had big, pageant queen blonde hair and some pregnancy weight on me. You and Lilja were such a celebrity couple at the time."

"Surely not. We'd been together quite a while before that."

"That's true. But nobody had seen you prior to that. Lilja was known for having her men wear a doctoral hat as a minimum requirement before she even looked at them. You were lucky to get rid of that cow in time." There was a sharpness in Jaana's voice.

"Was there some bad blood between the two of you?" Juho pried.

"Lilja was in the habit of telling me how well I played my cards, getting myself supported by a doctor with good income, only being a trained nurse. Lilja herself is an oncologist. She was hitting on Pasi hard and making him really uncomfortable."

Jaana was frowning, reminiscing about Lilja's escapades among doctors.

Juho was amazed at Jaana's straightforwardness. According to Juho's recollection, one of the requirements of Lilja, when it came to men, was good looks, and Pasi definitely didn't fit into that category.

Antti attended their bantering. This was the first time he was able to follow his partner's intimate relationships with women. He had met Lilja a few times at some party or another. She had the essence of a Valkyrie: very self-confident and looking at Juho's colleagues down her nose.

"Since I didn't come here to reminisce about the past, we might as well get straight to business." Jaana changed the subject as it was obvious that Juho had no desire to bring his personal issues into the workplace. Prior to having a mandatory coffee cup in front of her, Jaana cut to the chase: "Was there something specific you wanted to discuss?"

"Sanna told us about your evening out last week. We would like to talk with you as well on the subject. There might be something Sanna or Anu missed about the encounter," Juho started.

Jaana looked at them for a moment and burst into laughter: "Do you really think Sanna could forget something? That woman has the memory of an elephant. Any amount of alcohol has no impact on her. But it was quite an interesting encounter. The lads tried to impress us by bragging about their accomplishments. And doing some fishing on Mikael. Fortunately, they had no idea Pasi is my husband. If they had, there would have been no end to their questions. As if Pasi ever talks shop with me, anyway. There is one issue you might not have heard from Sanna. One of the boys was hitting on her, pretending he was serious. I found it truly weird. As if they had planned to do something to her. I just got a bad feeling about it," Jaana spoke with passion. It was obvious there was worry for her friend's well-being in her voice.

"Did you discuss it afterwards together?" Juho picked up on the subject.

"Sanna and Anu agreed with me. Although Sanna laughed at it, we could see it made her feel uncomfortable. Maybe she got some kind of premonition or something. Sanna is very sensitive that way."

"You were right when you said that she didn't mention it before; I confronted her about it last night. Sanna claimed to have been too tired to continue the night any further," Juho stated. "You complimented Sanna's memory just now, but didn't she have some memory loss after her collision?" he went on.

"Yes, she did lose that one week completely. Since then, Sanna's memory has worked better than the two of ours combined."

"She said that back then, it was easy to convince her about the events during the blackout."

"If you mean your brief visit to the hospital, that is true in a way, but it was us being on the wrong side of things," Jaana smiled, recalling the past.

"What did you mean about the premonitions?" Antti jumped in.

"Sanna sees things we cannot. She calls it chills. For example, when I was pregnant for the first time, she knew it before I did. She also knows when somebody is bullshitting." Jaana cut her speech short and looked straight into Juho's eyes with wide-eyed astonishment. "I am really slow today. Does this mean that you and Sanna..." she gasped. "So, when did this happen? Why was I kept in the dark again?"

"Well, I had a very nice chat with Sanna the night before last. We discussed her amnesia and other stuff. I just realised what's been bugging me ever since. Sanna lost her memory in that accident. Can it be implemented with a drug?" Juho wanted to take the discussion onto safer waters.

"Yes, that's how knock-out drops usually work," Jaana nodded.

"Are they easy to access in your experience?" Juho went on.

"It depends on what you want to use them for. For example, you can buy them in any pharmacy, providing you have a prescription. And the doctors are more than willing to give them to anyone with a good story. I've heard of them being distributed around the university campus as well."

"Have you ever had a professional encounter with knockout drops?"

"I used to work in the Psychiatric Clinic before this enterprising stuff. The cases came around there with a slight delay. That is when the victims got flashbacks of the abuse. You guys never get to investigating them around here. After a few years, it's difficult to find any evidence of the event. At any rate, if the victim doesn't remember the incident…" Jaana talked seriously.

She could recall at least a couple of cases from the Psychiatric Clinic. Both were girls having symptoms of depression emerging quite suddenly before they had been admitted to the hospital, after multiple suicide attempts. Jaana had already started at Ex Tempore when she heard one of the girls was successful in her last attempt. These cases had touched her deeply due to the girls' lives being destroyed completely because of one reckless night. Afterwards, Jaana had done voluntary work among the rape victims and talked in different sectors of schools about the subject.

"Basically, drugging somebody is a crime in itself, let alone the other stuff that comes with that. As you all very well know. You can feed false memories to a person since the sense of time goes as well as the memory. Sanna didn't have any idea how long she had been in the hospital after her accident," Jaana cleared the issue.

Juho and Antti nodded at her words.

"That's how I comprehended the situation. She said about not having any recollection of the incident," Juho replied to her.

They finished the conversation soon after that. Antti escorted her downstairs. As they were departing, Jaana wished them good luck, with a twinkle in her eye.

Juho and Antti decided to take their lunch break after her departure, before Ville's and Antero's status check. When they arrived at the canteen, it was almost packed full. After they had filled their trays and were looking for a free space, Juho spotted a twosome sitting at the table by the window. They sat on the free chairs. Saying his greetings, Juho pondered if he should ask them about the drug connections at Utopia he had enquired about the previous week. Maarit Vartiainen and Valtteri Kallio were both experienced narcs. Both knew the underworld of Oulu like the back of their hands.

Maarit smiled at Juho mischievously: "Have you already caught your killer? Sorry, we couldn't find the female you were looking for."

"We haven't nicked anyone yet, but we're getting closer every minute. That woman appears to be one of our suspect's attempts to distract us," Juho replied with the same tone.

"Little birds have sung to us that you two have had a lot of female company recently," Maarit continued.

"Believe it or not, most of them are drug dealers," Antti cracked in the middle.

His comment raised a burst of well-earned laughter among the table group. Antti answered Maarit's and

Valtteri's pries dryly that their selling ventures were strictly legal, although it sounded a bit weird.

"Seriously speaking, we got a slightly different story from your colleagues in Helsinki. Olli Simanainen called us, worried, revealing to us that the lady in question had informed them about that pot plant in the Marjaniemi allotment. She had, by accident, heard the guy talking about it just before she made him hit the road," Juho clarified to their new patterns.

"Those two guys became real living legends in the narc world. And now you are telling us that they opened the case with just a stroke of dumb luck. Did she tell you why she broke up with him?"

"She said that she wasn't going to give her widow's mites to the business ventures of just a fuck buddy," Juho replied, word for word from what Olli had told him.

Maarit shook her head, astonished by Sannas's blunt words. Continuing the debate, Juho asked all of them what they thought the pharmacist did for a living. When none of them found the right answer, Juho replied curtly: "They just give in and put out all day."

This made the whole table group burst into frantic laughter, catching the attention of the whole canteen.

Maarit asked if Juho had heard something similar about policework.

Juho replied, smiling: "The police just take in and put out."

This made Maarit and Valtteri shake their heads and they thanked him for brightening their day.

Juho accepted their thanks, trying to look modest.

On her way out, Maarit threw a line: "Good luck with your putting out! Don't take in too much!"

Once they returned upstairs, they carried on checking the alibis of the boys. Ville and Antero had come back enthusiastically from their snack bar round but refused to reveal anything else before they had shown their findings from the saved hard drive file of the Kino Grilli to Juho and Antti.

They watched it anxiously until Juho stopped the recording on two images on the screen. After a short silence, Juho shrieked: "Busted!" and gave Antti a high five.

At the end of the day, they scheduled their moves for starting off the next morning. The boys would be picked up at dawn for further interrogation. This time, they should come clean.

They made a list of all their questions together. Their aim was to make the boys sweat unless the truth was coming up. Having finished everything, Ville went downstairs to make arrangements, fetching the boys at 7am and booking three interrogation rooms in order to keep them apart for the whole time.

As Juho was driving home, he went through the results of the day, trying to figure out if some small detail had managed to slip through the gaps. Even after contemplating the whole evening, he was certain of their watertight plan. When calling Sanna, he didn't mention anything about the case, keeping the chat as light as possible.

TWENTY

ON FRIDAY, SANNA TOOK the bus to and from work as usual. She did her weekend grocery shopping in Halpa-Halli in Meri-Toppila. There was not a lot of it, mostly breakfast ingredients for the next morning. The rest of the meal plans she left for Juho.

On Saturday morning, she slept in. She made herself breakfast after waking up, and then emptied her head in front of the TV. As the clock was nearing to midday, Sanna decided to make herself a couple of cups of coffee, since she hadn't heard anything from Juho. Just when she had poured her first mug, her phone rang. There was Juho's name on the screen, making Sanna wonder if telepathy did really exist.

Juho's first words were: "I am calling still at work. It might take a couple more hours before we can make a weekend getaway. I just wanted to let you know so you don't think I'm standing you up."

"Are you doing me an Ostrobothnian foreplay – in other words – think of yourself wet; I'll be home in an hour?" Sanna laughed.

"Here we go again with those big girls' talks! I don't want you getting started on anything before I get there," Juho said strictly, with laughter in his voice.

While he was still speaking, he heard Sanna's doorbell ringing. Sanna had apparently noticed it as well, since she sighed: "If you think that it is a good joke to say that you are still at work and now you are behind my door, you might face being a sexless innkeeper this weekend!"

"Sanna! I swear and assure you I'm still sitting behind my office desk here in Raksila."

"We'll soon find out when I open the door and see who's behind it, won't we?"

"Okay. Don't cut me off just yet; we could chat a bit before my break ends," Juho reminded Sanna.

She put her phone on the kitchen countertop and rushed to the door. The ringer had started to sound impatient. Her surprise was genuine when she saw Topi standing behind the open door.

"Oh, hi! Isn't it Topi? Was that your name? How did you find your way here?"

"Hi, and my apologies for disturbing you like this! Sarita gave me your address and I decided to come and have a chat with you due to my concerns about her state of mind. I think she is taking it pretty hard."

Sanna opened the door wide before asking him to walk into the apartment.

Topi went into the hallway, leaving Sanna to close the door. Topi's words about Sarita set her alarm bells off. Sarita had never been the least interested in her place of residence. So, she just instinctively turned the door lock into an open position. At least she could exit quickly should she need to.

As she was still fumbling with the door, Topi had advanced to her living room. He looked around with curiosity: "It seems you weren't expecting me here? Were you disappointed since I wasn't your boyfriend?"

Sanna blurted at him, astonished: "What boyfriend are you referring to? I'm still single."

Topi looked at her, his head tilted.

"I heard somewhere that you are quite close to one of the coppers."

"And what kind of equestrian news agency did that information come from?" Sanna puffed.

"I cannot recall who told me about it. Maybe it was just a misunderstanding. But let's talk about Sarita. That being the reason I'm here."

"Okay. Want some coffee? I just made it for myself but there is enough for you as well," Sanna talked, while walking towards the kitchen.

Passing her phone, she quickly glanced at it, making sure that Juho was still on the line.

"My doors are always open to Sarita's friends, after all. Especially if Sarita is in a bad place. Sit down! We may as well do the talking in here. Maybe we can sort her things out."

Topi thanked her for the coffee offering, noticing it was a strong, dark roasted variety. Sanna asked him if he was taking milk in his coffee as she set the full mug on the table. When Topi said yes and she turned her back to him in order to get the milk out, he emptied the contents of a small syringe he held in his hand into Sanna's coffee. Sanna laid the milk carton on the table.

They compared the quality of hospital coffee and the dark roasted one for a while, until Sanna changed the subject to Topi's original issue. He began his tale of Sarita being under the weather and Aleksi making passes at her. He insinuated that Aleksi had done the same to Sanna.

Sanna laughed at him, saying that she was familiar with the student pranks from her nursing days, before any of the lads had even thought about being doctors. As Sanna went on with the conversation, she told Topi that she was quite certain of the fact that the whole story about Aleksi stealing the refined spirits belonged to the same category, unless he proved to be a criminal mastermind, avoiding the police getting a clue as to how he had done it. At this point, Topi burst into laughter and bragged how he had managed to con everybody with a couple of empty spirits bottles and Polish vodka he had brought home as a souvenir. Everything went hunky-dory on his part. Sanna was the only one seeing through his trickery so far.

Sanna pondered out loud why Topi hadn't talked about Sarita's issues with his friends. She was a total stranger to the girl, after all. The oddity of the whole situation bothered her more and more. Topi said that neither of them had answered his calls. They seemed to have vanished into thin air. Topi continued on the same subject, suspecting them to be involved in Mikael's murder and having bolted.

While Topi kept on beating around the bush, Sanna started feeling really weird. Topi's voice wavered oddly in her ears. Concentrating her thoughts was harder and harder by the minute, and she felt a strange tingling sensation in her muscles. Sanna peeked in her coffee mug as if there was something added to the bottom of it. She breathed fiercely and blurted out: "Did you idiotic motherfucking son of a bitch put something in my coffee?"

Topi looked at her, astonished.

"Where have you got that idea? Are you feeling somewhat different, faint or tired? Let me get you to rest a while." He tried to calm Sanna down following her reaction to the diazepam he had added to her coffee.

There was no sign of drowsiness in her. On the contrary, she looked like she could run a marathon. It made him wonder if he had filled his syringe with the wrong stuff. Her pupils were like needlepoints but that was the only visible sign on the outside. Topi tried to recollect from their lectures on pharmacology if Sanna's reaction was something he should have been prepared for. Topi had never experienced this before. At this point, Sanna should have been drowsy. Topi pondered how he could get Sanna to calm down, since he wanted to carry out his well-constructed plan to frame Sanna as the culprit, with well-planted fake evidence. Sanna's disappearance would seal the deal.

Being frightened of Sanna's behaviour, Topi stood up. He tried to grab Sanna's waving hands in order to restrain her anxious movements, but she avoided his efforts.

"Was this how you got your mates to give you an alibi after Mikael's murder? Did Mikael catch you red-handed?"

"That idiotic Sarita happened to take a sip from the wrong glass. Mikael really freaked out and swore to catch the culprit and hold him accountable. That Sunday, I joined him at the pharmacy, supposedly to help him out. Consequently, we were going to make a plan to catch Aleksi red-handed."

"You had a good plan going back then. What went wrong?" Sanna was out of breath trying to talk and keep herself out of Topi's grasp.

"At the pharmacy, Mikael told me he knew my game was up. If I didn't come clean with the police, he would. He claimed to have all the evidence stashed away at home. That's why I stayed there overnight, sleeping on Sarita and Matias's sofa. Lucky me! I had already been able to convince the lads of your culpability. Hence, Aleksi tried to hit on you so hard. We were supposed to take you to Utopia or someplace else without your friends." Topi's temper was wearing thin.

"Why did you come here?" Sanna wondered.

"When you disappear and coppers find all the evidence here, we all go free. All of them are so stupid, believing everything I made up about your drug trafficking. After all, I am a future doctor, and you are just a dumbass bitch getting involved in police investigations in order to cover your criminal activities."

His words hit Sanna like a ton of bricks. Topi was telling the truth. Sanna was in a very vulnerable position in the eyes of a teenage boy with an inflated sense of self-importance. Even for Sanna herself, Topi's tale sounded believable. She felt the world crumbling down in front of her eyes. At the same time, a silent voice inside of her whispered that he was just stalling for time.

Sanna had circled the table, out of Topi's reach. She was making an effort to slip away to wider spaces, straight to the hallway and out of the flat. At that point, her phone and Juho at the end of the line had slipped out of her mind completely.

Topi had rotated around the table with Sanna while he was talking, stopping her from fleeing. When he thought that she was on the right spot behind the table, he jumped, using a chair as his stepping stone, over the table to get to Sanna. Or that was his plan. As he stretched from the seat of the chair, it collapsed under him. Sanna fell and jammed her right hand under the heavy tabletop. She was lucky since Topi had got stuck between the fallen table and the base of a cupboard. Before he was able to free himself, Sanna had managed to break out of the table's remains and head off to the hallway. Unfortunately, Sanna's speed didn't give her enough of a head start. Topi caught her in the kitchen doorway. His hold on Sanna's shirt tail didn't stop her proceeding but threw her against a mirror hanging on the wall, loosening it off the hooks so that it fell almost on top of her. The collision had luckily made Topi lose his grip on Sanna and she was able to half crawl to the sitting room. Topi had stood up and rushed to get his hands on some tool from a knife block on the counter before he followed Sanna.

Sanna was also standing up, looking for something she could use as a weapon. There was nothing apart from her laptop on the coffee table. She grabbed it without thinking what she was going to do with it. Her strength was wearing out. A small voice in the back of her head kept her at least somewhat composed, in spite of the weakness of her right hand hindering her. She held the laptop close to her chest and started off running towards Topi. Getting one meter away from him, she cast it at his head. He got confused by the flying object, giving Sanna just enough time to sneak out past him into the hallway.

Topi's confusion did not last more than a second. Having stopped the flyer with his hand, he turned immediately after Sanna. Reaching the door, Sanna flung it open, and at the same moment, Topi caught her. Sanna fell onto the corridor floor as Topi tackled her, almost perfectly, by putting his arms around her waist. They slid forward together on the slippery floor for almost two meters, before hitting the top of the stairwell. They continued their trip down the stairs, still attached to each other. During their somersault, Topi managed to hold on to his knife. When he rose it, someone wearing blue overalls grabbed his knife-hand from the wrist and twisted it until he was forced to drop the weapon. In a jiffy, both his hands were held back by a man standing behind him, preventing him from moving them. More policemen emerged, handcuffed him and whisked him into a Black Maria waiting outside.

Sanna stayed lying on the floor, eyes tightly shut. She felt like there was a hornet's nest planted inside her head. She wondered why Juho shook her shoulders and whispered odd words in her ear. For some reason, she found it really hard to concentrate on his voice. In the end, she was able to hear what Juho kept repeating. It just didn't make any sense to her.

"Sanna, darling! Are you all right? Please, say something! Don't you dare die now!"

"Stop babbling; I have no intention of dying. My stamina is not what it used to be. Please do lift me up before we end up under this collapsing house."

She had opened her eyes but was forced to close them again due to everything spinning around. After a while, the world seemed to be settling and staying in one place momentarily.

"What the fuck were you thinking taking the scenic route from Raksila?"

She saw the laughter in Juho's eyes when he answered: "Sanna, it is now half past twelve. It didn't take too long to get here. Your sense of time is a bit confused. The drugs Topi gave you might have caused it. Let me take you back to your flat."

He lifted Sanna gently in his arms and carried her up the stairs. At the end of the hallway, he glanced into the kitchen. It was in chaos. The table was shattered on the floor and fragments had flown around. The mirror that used to be hanging on the wall between the hallway and the living room lay broken on the floor. Beside the doorway was also a fragmented laptop. Juho walked cautiously over the shrapnel and sat down on the leather armchair, still holding Sanna in his arms. Sanna's right arm drooped limp on her lap, the left one she had wrapped around Juho's neck.

Sanna took a closer look at Juho.

"Did Topi hit you too or what happened to your eye?"

"No, I just didn't have time to dodge when you wrenched the door open at such a speed. It is nothing to worry about. What happened to your arm?" Juho asked worriedly.

"Oh, this? It got stuck under the table, twisting oddly. It can't be broken since my fingers move but the strength is all gone," Sanna reassured him.

"By the way, how did the table fall apart?"

"Topi tried to jump over it but he fell short a bit. When such a big guy landed on it like a sack of cement, it is no wonder it went into bits and pieces. I was lucky he didn't fall on top of me," Sanna bemoaned.

"Can I come with you to the hospital? The medics should be here any minute."

"Of course, you can. You might need some stiches on your forehead, anyway. You'll get a hansom black eye as a memory of today. We can then compare the colour of our bruises."

"Is the drug still having an effect on you? You are shaking as we speak."

"I think it is wearing off. I am getting after shakes from the whole hullabaloo. I wouldn't mind a little nap. Could you do me a favour? I would be very grateful," Sanna looked at Juho pleadingly.

"Of course! That's the least I can do. If it's possible," Juho replied.

"It's not that hard. All you have to do is to call my brother Alpo when we get to the hospital. It's better if you make the call. I just have no strength to talk to anyone."

Sanna was certain of his capability to tell the bad news in a calming way. Juho gave her hug to seal the deal.

The medics rushed in from the open front door. They glanced at the kitchen, astonished at the total mayhem. Next, they turned to take a look at the living room. Seeing Juho and Sanna, one of them blurted laconically: "It seems to me that Seppä has been a busy boy redecorating the whole place, am I right or what?"

He eyed Juho with anger.

Fortunately, Sanna had the sense to open her mouth before Juho's reputation was ruined forever.

"You're all wrong. Juho is my knight in shining armour, taking down the villain with his sword."

The medics glanced at Sanna, surprised. Then they shrugged and started to take a closer look at Sanna's and Juho's injuries. After the triage, they were taken to the hospital to get patched up. Sanna was quite content resting on the gurney in the back of the ambulance, Juho sitting by her side.

TWENTY-ONE

AT THE HOSPITAL, SANNA was whisked away to be X-rayed, whereafter she had to wait for the doctor to arrive. Juho sat there with her. Having phoned Alpo, he was called away by the nurse in order to get his laceration stitched. The nurse asked who had hit him. As Juho gave her a truthful reply that he got banged by a door, the nurse laughed and said: "That's what they all say!"

Juho burst out laughing as well, while waiting for the local anaesthetic to kick in. The doctor sutured his brow and gave him a medical report on the occupational accident. In addition, he ordered a week's sick leave so that Juho had no need to freak out his colleagues with his rainbow-coloured face. When Juho got back to Sanna, her arm had already been set right. She looked sleepy, and when Juho enquired about it, she responded that she'd got some really good stuff before the operation. Sanna wondered if her brother was coming to see her today. Juho nodded.

Soon, they could hear a man's voice from the corridor, asking for Sanna Blinck. Juho went to meet him. After the introduction, Juho wanted to have a private word with him before seeing Sanna's injuries. A few minutes later, they arrived at her bedside. She greeted her brother with a warm smile and a hug. They went on to discuss how they should communicate with their parents about today's events. Juho stood by, listening to them. When they had cleared the matters up between them, Alpo turned his attention to Juho.

"By the way, did Sanna have something to do with that wound of yours?"

"I stood behind the door when Sanna flung it open. Why so?"

"Just thinking. If you have planned more close contact with my kid sister, I can lend you my extra jockstrap and helmet," Alpo stated with a straight face.

There was, on the other hand, an amused glimmer in his eyes, making it difficult for Juho to decide whether he was serious or not.

"That is my political opponent's false propaganda. It was all your own fault," Sanna protested from her bed.

"That's what you always say," Alpo snorted back. "I'll leave you two alone for a moment. I'll call Mother and try to stop her flipping, as she usually does where Sanna is concerned."

He dug his phone from his pocket, exiting the room.

"Could you come a little nearer? I need some TLC," Sanna said to Juho, patting her bedside with her able hand. He sat in the designated place.

"I am still huggable if you're wondering," Sanna cooed, pulling Juho nearer her.

Juho did what she asked. "Did Topi break any of your ribs?"

"As a matter of fact, he didn't, but I managed to get really cool bruising. Wanna see?"

Juho nodded and she pulled the shirt tail of her hospital pyjama top up to under her breasts. On the side, there were two large bruises almost on top of each other. Juho caressed the bruise until he heard Sanna's breathing getting heavier.

"I'm sorry; I didn't mean to cause you any pain," he said, pulling his hand away.

"I should be the one apologising since I spoiled your weekend."

"And I had planned all kinds of fun for us. I even bought a double sleeping bag for my tent in Nallikari," Juho replied in the same light tone.

"Wow! You have really made an effort. Your job as a security man is terminated at this point."

"I wasn't planning on doing any security jobs. We do have some mutual interests."

"Like what?"

"You told me that you like eating and fucking as well as I do."

"We are skipping both of them today, anyway."

"What's happening next?"

"I will be transferred to the ward at least for one night. You probably need to go to work to do the things you are so good at."

"No, I meant for the two of us. Can I come visit you once you get to the ward later today or tomorrow?"

"You can do whatever you want. You know well enough where I am."

Juho chuckled, hugged Sanna and kissed her passionately on the mouth.

"I think I should go now before they throw me out due to inappropriate conduct," Juho laughed and let go of Sanna.

In the corridor, he met Alpo, still holding his mobile phone to his ear. When he noticed Juho, he waved his hand at him to come closer. He pressed the phone on his chest and whispered: "Could you say something soothing to my mother? She doesn't believe me saying Sanna is all right. She's probably planning a funeral or something like that already."

Alpo passed the phone to Juho. When the latter introduced himself, her flow of words diminished for a minute, starting off her bemoaning again. He managed to calm her down by going through all the day's events, step by step. Mama Terttu admitted to flipping out for nothing as she was having a flashback of Sanna's car accident. She kept on talking, making it difficult for Juho to end the call. He had to plead being busy at work before Terttu went silent, wishing him a good weekend.

He pondered to Alpo about Terttu's hysterical reaction when she heard of Sanna's misfortune. Alpo responded that she had been like that ever since Sami died. Their mother expected the worst, as Sanna fought for her independence in blood and soul. Alpo had to be the middleman due to both sides relying upon his neutrality. Their dad tried to do his bit in restraining her guardianship, with varying degrees of success. Juho asked him if Sanna had always been as willing to look after others, regardless of her own well-being. Alpo gave it a bit of thought before responding that it had been like that ever since Sami passed away. As if she had given up on a life of her own.

"Will you send me a message with her ward and room number? I'll try to see her tonight. I suppose I'll have to get a cab back to work."

"I can give you a lift to Raksila. It's the least I can do. After all, you might just have saved Sanna's life today. I'll go tell her where I'm going, so she won't get worried."

As Alpo got back, they went to the car park and stepped into the car. Juho asked: "What was the thing about the jockstrap being needed? It sounded like an inside joke."

It made Alpo burst into laughter, reminiscing about his past.

Juho took a closer look at him, trying to find a resemblance between the siblings. Alpo's hair was darkish blond and cut short. His eyes were brown. On his facial expression, he saw similarities with Jasper Pääkkönen's boyish charm. He wondered which one of the siblings took after their mother and which after their father.

Alpo started his tale about their summer together in a rented summer cottage in Inari. Sanna and Alpo had to spend a lot of time together. They were lucky to have a stack of comic books to read. In one of them were pictorial instructions on how to repel an attack. Of course, it had to be tested in situ right away. Two seconds later, Alpo had found himself wriggling on the floor, with his hands on his groin. Sanna stood beside him, her eyes big as a plate, and wondered what had happened to her brother. It was pure luck their parents had been at the supermarket, having no idea what had occurred during their absence.

Juho burst into laughter. Alpo tried to ease him back; it was not the whole story. The next week, their parents had decided their kids needed some other things to do besides being inside the cottage and took them to the nearby playing field. There, they found a baseball bat, a ball and a couple of baseball mitts. The game was started with two-person teams. On Sanna's turn at batting, Alpo had started to chaff her about her loose strikes until his sister got seriously angry with him and yanked a fastball towards her brother. Alpo had thought he could catch it but his estimation of its trajectory was a bit off. And of course, it hit him straight on his forehead. Alpo had lost consciousness, regaining it at the village health centre.

At this point, Juho wriggled with laughter. In between his bursts, he lamented how hard Alpo's childhood must have been. Alpo laughed back that this wasn't the worst part; his mummy dearest had lashed out at him out for teasing his little sister. Juho was still wiping tears from his eyes as they arrived at the yard of the police house.

In his workplace, Juho barged straight in to talk to his boss, Kyösti Raappana. As he handed in his medical report, Raappana took a closer look at his injuries and stated that Juho was allowed to start his sick leave after writing his report on the day's incidents.

Juho told him that he'd recorded the entire call on his mobile phone, giving them enough basis to go straight to the scene in order to detain Topi. What he did not reveal was the fact that he hadn't recorded the entire phone call, only part of it. Kyösti took notes while they were listening to the recording. He intended to ask Topi for some clarification of the events. They agreed on Antti and Kyösti visiting Sanna in the hospital at some point on Sunday, providing she was up to it. Kyösti admitted that Juho was right about Sanna's interrogation abilities. She had, after all, made Topi tell a full account of the events of the fateful Sunday evening.

Juho did his paperwork for the rest of the afternoon. His workmates popped in for a chat, just to see his black eye and stitches. He anticipated there would be some betting going on as to the size and colour of the bruise. Juho himself couldn't be bothered to look in the mirror unless he had to go to the toilet. When the anaesthetic was wearing off, he could feel a throbbing pain on his eyebrow. In the end, he got a disposable ice pack from the medicine cabinet, pressing it to his forehead. Later on, Kyösti brought Topi's statement, confessing everything from killing Mikael to Sanna's attempted murder. Juho realised after reading it how quickly Sanna had deducted every event. A lot quicker than any of them. He asked if Kyösti intended to tell Sanna about his confession when visiting her. Kyösti replied that he was going to mention the main points of it, although Sanna knew most of them after Topi's attack on her.

TWENTY-TWO

IT WAS ALMOST DUSK when Juho finished his report, allowing him to leave. He visited the hospital cafe, before going to the ward, to purchase the tabloids Alpo recommended and an additional *Seven* magazine. Having also grabbed a Fazer's Blue chocolate slab, he counted on doing his best to make sure Sanna's stay in the hospital would be as comfortable as it could be. When he arrived at Sanna's room, he found her sound asleep, holding the TV remote in her hand. He pulled a chair to Sanna's bedside, trying to stop it making any sound. He took the remote from Sanna's hand and turned the TV off.

Juho sat peacefully by her side, holding her hand. Once or twice, he tried to free it, but Sanna wouldn't let him. Juho didn't have the heart to use force to get it off, since he had nowhere else to go. He had asked the nurses on his arrival the exact time he had to make his departure from the ward. The visiting hours ended at 8pm, so when the time was getting nearer, he leant into Sanna and said quietly to her: "I have to leave now before they throw me out."

Sanna opened her eyes slightly: "As always."

"I'll be back tomorrow at a better time."

Sanna nodded: "You can do what you want. Can I get a goodnight kiss or are you too busy for that?"

"Never too busy to kiss you."

Sanna gave a sleepy smile and wrapped her left arm around Juho's neck. She pulled Juho down until their lips touched. The kiss seemed to last a small eternity before Sanna let Juho go, caressed his cheek and nestled deeper under the blanket. Juho turned off the lights and told the nurses at the station that Sanna had gone to sleep. They promised to go check on her during the evening.

On Sunday morning, Sanna woke up refreshed by her long sleep. It was too early for the nurses or any of the staff to start the morning routines. She contemplated the events of the previous day. All of a sudden, Sanna remembered her dream of Juho sitting by her bedside and holding her hand. It felt very real, as dreams often do. The peace of the holy morning prevailed in the room. The bed next to her was made with clean bedclothes, waiting for a new resident to arrive. Sanna pushed the button which elevated her bed. Her eyes caught the newspapers and on the top of them, a slab of Fazer's Blue on the table. On the top of the stack seemed to be a handwritten note.

'Honey, you wanted to rest your eyes so badly, I had to let you get some sleep. I'll come back in the daytime, when you are more alert. Regards, Juho. P.S. Former "dream man", now "future real man".'

Sanna smiled contentedly, realising Juho had really been there for her. She placed the tabloids on her lap one at a time. She had just begun to read the Evening News as the orderly brought her breakfast. With the same door opening came the nurse, carrying a medicine tray. Sanna was glad to see her, since every move she made with her right arm sent bolts of lightning through her whole arm.

"I heard you had a gentleman caller here last night. Were you both injured in the same fight? I hope it was all right letting him in. I mean, him having a black eye too." The nurse, called Saara, was concerned. "I mean, it wasn't a domestic dispute, was it?" she pried.

"Not in the least. As a matter of fact, he is a copper. He and his mates saved my life. I flung the door open straight into Juho's eye trying to escape from the attacker. He can come here anytime. It's nice to have company since I don't have a roommate to talk with."

"As you know, things can change really quickly. You'll be on your own until we need the spare bed. Anneli Kantelinen was the night nurse last night and she told me that you have a lot of acquaintances here due to working in theatres and other places. She sent you her regards. And promised to pay you a visit when she comes for her night shift."

Sanna finished her breakfast slowly after Saara's exit and got out of bed cautiously. Her trip to the toilet went without a hitch, one-handed. She scrutinised her face while washing her hands. Her right cheek was swollen and colourfully bruised. She palpated it with her hand, feeling how tender it was, but luckily the skin hadn't broken. The bruises would fade away in a few days. She ran her fingers through her hair and decided to have her morning stroll to the common room of the ward, hoping to get another cup of coffee and

Sunday's *Kaleva*. As it happened, she found both of them. Fortunately, somebody had already made coffee. Two cups later, she decided to go back to her room to read in peace.

Sanna got her first visitors after lunch. Antti came with Kyösti Raappana to take her statement. On the arrival of the men, Sanna was sitting on the top of her bed, one leg bent and the other hanging casually on the side of the bed, browsing the tabloid and watching TV. She folded the paper and turned off the telly the minute they emerged. She apologised for her left-handed greeting due to her right hand being supported by an angular splint and a sling.

"Are you aware that Juho recorded the entire assault on his phone, starting from Topi coming in?" Kyösti began.

Sanna looked at them, astonished.

"No, I didn't. I was busy staying alive at that point." Sanna shook her head thoughtfully.

She went on talking about her experience the day before. Everything seemed to go haywire after the benzos started to kick in. Topi had explained enthusiastically about Utopia, but the whole point went over her head. Antti enlightened her that Topi had stated to them that Sanna was in charge of drug and girl trafficking, based in the mentioned nightclub's bar. Sanna looked at Antti with her mouth open, astonished. She pondered a moment, and then asked Antti to repeat what he had just said. Due to hearing it the second time, Sanna's face distorted with anger.

"Wow! You must have felt like you were getting an early Christmas with presents signed and sealed. Once again, one pill-popping pharmacist was busted by a bright-eyed med student. Getting the evidence must have been like a walk in the park. More gold and glory with medals on your chest as a result. The first thing you learnt was that I had a grip on Pasi's balls. Is there anything easier than for a woman to plead doctor-patient relationship in order to get mixed up in the inquiry from the beginning? And then the cherry on the cake: Olli phones from Helsinki and tells you a heartbreaking tale of a scolded widow revealing her dealer/boyfriend's businesses. Of course, she's planning to start off with a clean slate in another place through her own firm. Everything goes hunky-dory until the boss's son reveals everything to his mate. As if I was ever the hottest catch someplace like the meat market in the Utopia bar. I would be the one to pay for the company. But let's not get to the facts messing things up. I must have been a real criminal mastermind to conceal the evidence. Now, we have to put Plan B into action. Let's get the hottest hunk in the station to have a one-to-one meeting at the widow's apartment. And give him the authorisation to use every trick in the book to get a full confession. It was bad luck for him that one night was not enough. Maybe a weekend in some shitty love nest would reveal everything you needed. At that point, Juho must have started to chicken out and then somebody got the bright idea to give Topi a chance to be the hero of the hour. Which one of you eggheads gave birth to the idea of putting Topi on my trail?"

Antti tried to interpose but Sanna silenced him with a wave of her hand.

"There is nothing you can explain to me. You prejudged me from the beginning. I should have been able to figure out how far you were willing to go to prove yourselves right.

And now, you can all go to hell for all I care – I'm getting sick and fucking tired of you and your department." Sanna pulled her blanket higher, turned her back on the men and buried her face in her pillow.

Kyösti sat on his chair, dumbfounded. After considering a while, he rose to sit on the side of Sanna's bed and started patting her back soothingly: "Now, little lady, you should calm down. While you do that, Antti can explain what they have been up to. And if you still want to make an official complaint, I can begin the process."

"Sorry! I didn't mean it that way. I have no idea what's happening to me. Usually, I can contain myself better," Sanna's voice was subdued. She didn't lift her head.

Antti's face had blushed, listening to Sanna's tirade. He pondered how he should put his words without causing her to blow off again.

"You don't have to apologise to us. This has been a tough experience for you. We do have to examine all the tips we get. Although they seem to be really far-fetched. We had both seen you in action, both in Linnanmaa and in the autopsy. Have you been able to figure out what was bothering you with Matias?"

"I got it just last night. Matias's pupils were small as needlepoints. That made me first suspect an overdose. How did you get on Topi's trail? Or is it classified information?" Sanna had turned her face towards Antti. She rose up on her bed, leaning on her pillows and smiling reassuringly at both of them. Signs of tears were still visible on her face.

Antti felt relieved once Sanna's tantrum seemed to have died down. Kyösti had difficulty comprehending how Sanna could be a raving fury one moment and a pussycat slurping cream the next second.

Antti revealed that they had considered the possibility of the boys involvement as one of their lines of inquiry ever since they had interviewed Topi the first time. Breaking their alibis was another thing. Aleksi's neighbours had complained of the noise going on the whole night. Of course, nobody confronted him or called the cops, which was usual conduct when handling disturbances in Oulu. They had to rely on their word that none of them had left the flat the entire evening in question, until Sanna had told them about Matias mentioning the sausage and chips which had been eaten during the night. It was supported by Pasi's report of the stomach contents. After that fact, it was easy to clarify who had purchased their stodge. Topi had constructed a watertight plan. They had gone altogether to Aleksi's place to enjoy the first beers. Topi had spiked Aleksi's and Matias's drinks. Then, Mikael had announced he had to go to work and Topi had offered to help him. On the way, they had stopped at Kino Grilli to have a meal and were captured on the security cam. At the Third, they had discussed what Topi had been up to during their cleaning. Mikael had made his last demand to Topi that he give himself up to the police. Failing to do so, Mikael would take all the evidence he had gathered on a memory stick to the authorities himself. Topi hadn't found it from searching through Mikael's belongings at the pharmacy.

After completing his deed, he went back to the kiosk and bought another helping. That visit was also found from Grilli's hard drive. On his arrival back to Aleksi's flat, he convinced the others that he'd been away just for a quarter of an hour. Consequently, it was easy for him to get them to drink enough to be oblivious and pretend to be totally pissed himself. Juho and Antti had been able to figure it out, thanks to Sanna. She had mentioned how easy it had been to convince her that Juho's visit had been just a product of her imagination. To Topi's dismay, Matias had mentioned the sausage and chips. It was something Topi had found out when they had chatted in Street Cafe with Anu. After that, it had been easy to follow Sanna home and wait for the right moment to attack her. The moment had come on Saturday morning after he had seen the police taking Matias into custody. Topi hadn't realised how Sanna would react to his knock-out drops, which proved to be her lucky break. Topi's plan was to make her disappear and plant the evidence of her guilt in her apartment. He had no idea how clearly all the evidence the police had gathered pointed to him. They had never thought of using Sanna as bait; Topi's attack had been a total surprise to them. As a matter of fact, Juho had beaten himself up the whole way to Meri-Toppila for not having taken Sanna to safety already on Friday. Sanna's reaction to the knock-out drops had startled them all.

Sanna had listened to Antti's account, her eyes wide open: "Did you find out during your interview with Topi why he chose to drug the girls instead of charming them with his accomplishments? I mean, he is not mum's little angel anymore."

"Keeping it short, it started off when his high school girlfriend dumped him for another guy. It hurt his pride.

Accordingly, he drugged the girl and abused her. To top his vengeance, he sent the photos to her new boyfriend. In time, it became an obsession for him, to such an extent that he never even tried to get girls in a normal way. Later on, he got more satisfaction from having photos to remind him of his doings. We found everything on his computer," Antti clarified.

Kyösti had listened to Antti's account, nodding at appropriate points. As Antti got to Sanna's reaction, he asked more specific questions about what had happened in the flat after Sanna freaked out. Sanna confessed to having a similar reaction after her accident, when she was on her way to the operating theatre. The anaesthetist had given her diazepam as a premedication and she had tried to run away with her broken legs. Afterwards, she had been told that benzos were cut off from her list of medication permanently. She had no idea of it before the doctors mentioned it to her later on. As Sanna had realised that Topi had put something in her coffee and her whole system had gone into override, she had figured out the whole configuration. If Kyösti wanted to know more, he could google a pair of words: paradoxical reaction. Kyösti wrote it down. They started to take off and promised to stay in touch if they had more questions.

Just before their departure, Kyösti enquired as to when Sanna would be released from the hospital. Sanna replied that she had to stay there one more night, since Pasi had arranged a case study lecture in cooperation with the registrars, in the spirit of a teaching hospital.

As the men were walking to their car, Kyösti burst into laughter. Antti looked at him, pondering.

"From now on, we must get that hottest hunk of our department to interview all the female punters," Kyösti explained between his bursts.

Antti started a peal of relieved laughter.

Fortunately, Kyösti wasn't angry at them as a consequence of Sanna's words.

"Seppä has his hands full with his bride to be," Kyösti went on, driving back to work.

Antti had no choice but to agree with his boss's words.

TWENTY-THREE

IT WAS ALREADY LATE afternoon as Juho emerged from the glass door of the ward. He had bought a couple of orchids from the flower kiosk downstairs to cheer Sanna up. Walking past the lounge door, he saw a pissed-off-looking Anu sitting by the table.

"It is really nice to see you. You'll get some coffee if you come here for a minute. I really need someone in their right mind to talk to for a moment. Those fucking stalwart Taipale siblings are driving me barking mad," Anu cried out of the open door.

Juho glanced at her with astonishment.

"What's bugging you?"

"I'm most pissed off at it all. Sanna announced going straight home and wanting to be left alone. She won't manage there, but all Alpo has to say is that Sanna can do whatever she wants to do. It's all your fault anyway," Anu explicated, agitated.

"How come it's my fault? I have just tried to keep Sanna safe and healthy." Juho wanted to verify what he was hearing.

"Those colleagues of yours came to chat with Sanna. Apparently, she flipped out at them. Sanna is quite certain you don't have the guts to come anywhere near her ever again."

"Yeah, I heard the whole story. The guys were quite dumbfounded at Sanna's feedback but they have heard worse prior to this. They got lucky Sanna wasn't carrying any lethal weapons to enhance her words. Our boss was infatuated by her sparring with words. In his opinion, it was really invigorating to get such a sharp analysis of his subordinates' way of goofing around."

Anu started to pour coffee into three cups.

"I hope you don't think I am a horrible person because of this. I'll be all right in a minute," she went on as she saw Juho laughing inside.

"Why don't we make a deal that I take her up to my place tomorrow for a few days to recuperate. After all, we were going to spend the weekend together. But in order to make it happen, I need a favour from you: get Sanna some of her stuff and bring it to my place so there is no way she can make a fuss."

"That could actually work. Give me your address and leave the rest with me. But not a word to Sanna. She would go to the dogs otherwise," Anu warned.

Anu and Juho walked together to Sanna's room.

"Look who I found strolling down the corridor," Anu said as she set the coffee cups on the bedside table.

Sanna sat on her bed, legs crossed. Kneeling behind her was about a five-year-old girl, holding a hairbrush in her hand. She was so focused on brushing Sanna's hair that she kept it up even as she saw them enter. On the foot of the bed sat two nine-year-old girls, appearing to be twins. They were also concentrated on chatting and laughing with Sanna. It was obvious they were very close to each other. As Sanna saw Juho coming into the room, she patted the bed in front of her, waving him to sit there. Once he sat down, Sanna wrapped her good hand around his neck, pulled him closer and kissed him straight on his mouth.

Juho enjoyed the kiss, until he felt a tiny knock on his head and a small voice say, with a tight tone: "No kissing allowed. I'm tending to Sanna now."

Sanna laughed and reached out her hand, wrapping it around the little girl.

"You mustn't treat strange guys like that. I don't think you know that Juho is a policeman. And also, because of that, his head is already a bit booboo due to me knocking it."

The little girl glanced at Juho with widened eyes before saying: "Will he take us both to jail?"

"He is not taking us anywhere – he is a gentle sort of policeman," Sanna reassured her.

"I gave Juho that bruise, by the way, and he didn't get upset with me at all."

The little girl pondered Sanna's words for a moment, frowning.

"I thought that Sanna was here to get a baby, as Tuula from next door did."

None of the grown-ups had time to react to the sudden announcement as Juho heard one of the twins talking to her little sister: "How can you be so stupid, Ansku. Sanna cannot have babies due to her being a widow. Her hubby died a long time ago. Sanna won't get baby seeds anywhere anymore."

Ansku's lower lip was pushed forward. She had tears of anger in her eyes.

"Juho can give her those seeds. Then they could have a baby boy since our daddy can make only girls. Police must help people in need, as our daddy always says."

Sanna had followed Juho's facial expressions during the conversation. His face was blushed and the veins on his forehead bulged. His breathing sounded heavy. Suddenly, Juho stood up, with his hand over his mouth.

"I have to go to the toilet," he said to Sanna in a suffocated voice and rushed straight to the small powder room beside the door of the room. Sanna peered after Juho, surprised, at his departure. They listened to the strange noises coming from the toilet.

"What's wrong with him?" Sanna cried out to Anu, who was lying on the empty bed, jiggling with laughter.

"Go after him! I'll stay here and have a little chat with the girls."

Sanna knocked cautiously at the closed door before opening it. Inside, she saw Juho sitting on the toilet seat, his elbows on his knees, hands covering his face. From under his hands came strange noises.

"Are you hurt somewhere? Shall I call the nurse?" Sanna asked, frightened. She got nearer to Juho until she stood right in front of him. Suddenly, Juho jumped up and snatched her in his arms.

"You don't seem so transparent to me," he blurted out, laughing.

Sanna had no choice but to join in his joy. Occasionally, they tried to restrain their bursts of laughter, without success, until Sanna finally sighed and said: "Thank you for not laughing in front of the girls. I really didn't realise Ansku thought that you can take babies with you from the hospital. I thought you didn't want to have anything to do with me after I scolded you."

"It is no wonder if you lose your nerves from time to time. You went through the grinder yesterday. And it was actually very nice to hear that I am the hottest hunk in the department."

Juho set Sanna down to stand but didn't let her loose from his hug. They stood a moment, embracing each other, before going back to join the others.

The trio sat nicely on the edge of Sanna's bed. They looked embarrassed but shook hands with Juho, introducing themselves. The youngest one was Annamaija, usually called Ansku. The twins were Alina and Alisa. When the introductions were appropriately concluded, Ansku told them she wanted to carry on doing Sanna's hair. Juho sat beside her and began questioning her on her plans for Sanna's hair. Ansku admitted that all she knew how to do was comb and tie a ponytail. To Sanna's surprise, Juho asked Ansku if she wanted him to show her how to do a topknot. Being given permission, he collected Sanna's hair and tied it up with a rubber band. Then, he braided the ponytail, wrapped it around and tied it with another band. Having finished with the topknot, one of the girls passed Sanna a small mirror so she could see the result of Juho's work. Sanna examined her image for a moment and said to

Juho: "You are a multitalented man. Where did you learn to do that?"

"My sister is a hairdresser. She has a salon in Zepe. With the power of an older sister, she made her little brother coiffure her hair for her date nights."

"It hasn't been easy for you. Did your mates tease you a lot at school because of it?"

"They tried until they realised that I got lucky because of it."

There came a faint whisper behind Juho's back.

"Mummy, did he win a lot of money being lucky?" Ansku enquired curiously.

"It wasn't that kind of luck. The girls like boys who can make them look pretty and that's why it is called good luck," Anu replied absentmindedly.

"But Sanna's face still looks pretty awful. Can't Juho do something about it?"

"You mustn't say things like that! It upsets Sanna. We can now hit the road and give you two time to catch up." Anu tried to sound serious, despite a smile playing on the corners of her lips.

Anu went on collecting her daughters and her own paraphernalia scattered all over the room, resembling a bomb site.

"You should make that stalwart get some rest. Soon, she will start redecorating this room unless somebody keeps her occupied."

With these words, she left Sanna and Juho sitting on the bed. After a moment of silence, Sanna said: "I guess I didn't even thank you for the wonderful flowers. Today has been a real rollercoaster. I'm feeling a little knackered after all this buzz."

"Was that a subtle hint for me to make myself scarce and leave you in peace for the rest of the day? Should I leave, too?" Juho asked, pretending to be hurt.

"Of course not, silly. I did promise to show you all my magnificent bruises. And if you are a really good boy, you'll get the honour of buttering my bread. It is almost dinner time."

As Sanna was finishing her sentence, there was a knock on the door and the orderly emerged, carrying a tray. Juho helped her as best as he could. When the tray had been taken away and they had had their dessert coffees, Sanna lifted the head of the bed slightly and leaned against it.

"Will you come to enjoy the dusk beside me?"

"That's what I came for. But it was nice of you to ask."

Juho placed himself cautiously beside Sanna on the bed, wrapping his hands around her. He pulled Sanna's pyjama top upwards in order to see the bruises. Sanna turned on her belly and showed the marks on her back which had emerged after the fall on the stairs.

"This is like a map of a pagan land," he stated.

"And my face looks like a gargoyle from Notre Dame. I'm lucky to have a good hair day," Sanna replied, laughter in her voice.

"Then we make a good match," Juho smiled, pointing at his black eye.

Sanna pressed her head against Juho's chest and began rubbing her nose into it. Juho asked her quietly if she had ever thought about having a child of her own; she seemed to get along so well with her nieces.

Sanna continued moving her head on Juho's chest: "Do you want to hear the long version or the short one?"

"Long, of course; I am not going anywhere any time soon."

Sanna settled herself into a better position so she could see Juho's face as she was talking: "When Sami was still alive, everything was clear. We had agreed on having children after graduation. Then, everything backfired because of the collision. For years, I consoled myself that I was still young and had plenty of time. While waiting, I took care of my friends' children. Both of the Lampinen family babies had colic so I was a big help with them. I helped Anu and Alpo with the twins in the same way. And later on, I took in Ansku as my own. For each, I thought to myself that soon, it would be my turn. It just never happened. None of my former boyfriends asked even once whether I wanted to have children with them. Or with anyone for that matter. Since I have no desire to trick anyone to have a baby with me, the matter was dropped."

"That's crazy," Juho glanced at Sanna, astonished.

"It is not that odd if you come to think of it. I don't bring it up constantly. It is difficult to have children on your own," Sanna stated dryly.

"Have you thought about a sperm bank as an alternative?"

"Never! I want to have a child with a real human being. One who stays beside me through the pregnancy and all the other stuff. I just have never had the chance to try it in practice, so I have no idea if it's possible for me to get pregnant. What is your excuse for having no children?" Sanna's voice was irritated.

"I have a fifteen-year-old son; Samuli is his name. He lives in Kuusamo with his mother, stepfather and siblings. Back in the day when Marjut, ergo Samuli's mother, got pregnant, our relationship was hitting rock bottom. We tried to continue for the sake of our son but ended up just being flatmates with a child. Fortunately, we parted on good terms and I have been able to stay in his life ever since. Nevertheless, I have made up my mind to never again be a weekend father." Juho had clearly decided on the issue.

Sanna gave a deep sigh: "This is clearly not my day!"

"How come?" Juho pondered.

"I keep putting my feet in my mouth all the time. I should keep my bloody mouth shut."

Sanna snuggled nearer to Juho and began to move her good hand under Juho's shirt, kissing him passionately. They made love in silence, both listening out for sounds coming from the corridor. When the tea tray was brought in, they were lying in the bed, side by side, watching the telly, looking innocent. After the tea, Sanna walked Juho downstairs to the main entrance where they stayed for a while, embracing each other with no desire to let go.

"Do you want me to pick you up tomorrow when you're released?" Juho asked before leaving.

"I think I want some time to contemplate things on my own. If you really want, you can take me home, but I suppose I'm not fun to be around after all this. I have messed everything up."

Sanna had tears in her eyes.

TWENTY-FOUR

LATE ON MONDAY MORNING, Juho went back to the ward. He wanted to make sure he caught Sanna before she left. First, he stopped at the nurses station to make sure she was still there. When he got the affirmative, he headed to her room. Knocking the door and without waiting for an answer, he went in. At first, there was no one to be seen, but he was able to hear a subdued cursing and huffing behind the dividing curtain between the beds. He peeked in and saw Sanna fretting with her bra. He cleared his throat before saying: "Is that appropriate language for a respectable dowager?"

Sanna turned around towards him.

"If Mr Inspector sneaks into an honourable woman's boudoir in the middle of her dressing, you might hear something startling. Have you ever tried to put a bra on using one hand only? It would be interesting to hear you having a go with it."

"Clearly, I came in just the nick of time."

Juho took the bra from Sanna's hand, slid the straps in their place and closed the clasps on the back.

"Wait a bit now so I can adjust my boobs in right. It is not an easy task being one-handed."

"Sorry, I have no track record on that side. My experience consists only of taking them off," Juho stated gently.

"You still have to adjust your own package into the right place. Mine just happens to be on the top," Sanna snorted, supposedly offended.

Sanna went on getting dressed with help from Juho. Finally, she sat on the side of the bed. Sitting there, Sanna pondered how Juho had managed to time his arrival as she was leaving the hospital.

Juho sneered and said he suspected that Sanna wanted to run away with a young and sexy taxi driver if he didn't step in.

Getting her outdoor clothes on, Juho wondered at Sanna's woollen scarf, since it would be easier to handle a wool cap. Sanna's sharp response that a wool cap would make her look like a bubblehead made him laugh heartily. He kissed Sanna and said that she was beautiful on every occasion. The flowers Juho had brought were packed as carefully as Sanna's other stuff.

They left the hospital chitchatting. Juho's choice of route made Sanna wonder. Why was he taking a steady course on the motorway? In Sanna's opinion, going straight through the town to Meri-Toppila would have been quicker. Only when Juho drove past the crossing at Koskelantie, did Sanna begin to feel concerned.

Once they had turned at the Rajahauta crossing, they ended up in a carport in the courtyard of some small terraced houses. Sanna stayed put inside the car. Juho got out of the car and helped Sanna out.

"I thought you were taking me home. I don't live here."

"I didn't say to whose home I was taking you. Circumstantially, I happen to live here. I recall promising you the weekend together," Juho explained passionately, as if speaking to a child. "On the other hand, your pad needs a good cleaning up, so there is no chance you can rest there properly," he continued as they walked to the end of House B, where Juho opened the door, letting Sanna in first. At the entrance, he helped Sanna to take off her outdoor clothing and led her to sit on the corner sofa in the living room.

"I'll make us something to eat. You look a little peckish."

"Yes, thank you," Sanna breathed quietly.

She looked around for a while and said: "You have a nice-looking home here. Have you done the decor yourself?"

"As a matter of fact, I have. I moved here after Lilja emigrated to the States. We sold that apartment and I purchased this as a sort of bachelor pad."

"Yes, it is a good, peaceful place to bring women," Sanna noted, a bit relaxed now.

"If you really want to know the truth, you are the first woman I want to stay a while longer," Juho chatted from the kitchen, while preparing sandwiches.

"In other words, I am the first you have been able to capture here without resistance."

"We should inaugurate this shitty love nest properly, shouldn't we?" Juho chuckled.

Sanna stood up from the sofa and went around the peninsula, with cabinetry dividing the kitchen and living room. She wrapped her good hand around Juho's waist and rubbed her face on his back.

"I'm such an idiot. I don't understand how you can put up with me anymore. I have managed to botch up everything and still, you are so nice to me," Sanna began.

"We all botch things up once in a while. Besides, I should also think of my doings, since I hijacked you here without asking whether you wanted to come. It seemed such a good idea at the time."

"I didn't mean it like that. I would have probably come here, anyway. There is no way I could have gone home due to it being like a disaster zone. This just came unsuspectedly. I don't even have a change of clothes with me. As a matter of fact, I planned to have a shower first thing when I got home to wash the hospital smells off," Sanna explained her behaviour.

Juho turned and wrapped his arm around her shoulders. He set the sandwich plate on the dining table, with his other hand pulling Sanna to sit on a chair and then sat across the table.

Sanna grabbed a sandwich into her hand and began to gnaw it, deep in her thoughts.

Additionally, Juho snatched a wine bottle from the fridge and poured them a glass. Sanna tasted her wine and sighed: "Lambrusco. How did you know it's my favourite? You really made an effort on my coming here."

"One has to try to keep up one's reputation as the hottest hunk," Juho winked.

Sanna rested her elbow on the table and covered her eyes: "How long did it take you to make that up?"

Juho burst into laughter: "I just couldn't resist. Truth be told, I already bought it on Friday as I did some grocery shopping, anyway."

Sanna sighed and looked at Juho, frowning: "You look somewhat different today."

"I went to have a haircut at my sister's – maybe that has something to do with it."

"No, it's not that. Today you have been present in body and soul," Sanna commented and went on: "At first, when you were just present in body, I took it personally. Just before the autopsy, I realised how many cases like that you handle in your job. If you let them all get under your skin, you would find yourself in Oulunsuu psych ward in no time."

"That's one way of looking at it. In my mind, you have always been present in the soul, even when not in the body. Doesn't it balance things at least a bit? You took the initial situation with such confidence, making us almost crap our pants," Juho clarified his thoughts.

Sanna gazed at him, wondering how wrong one could be: "On the way home, I was at the point of explosion. I wanted to shout and rage at you two being so full of it. Fortunately, I'm no good at getting into hysterical fits in front of strangers. But I haven't made a habit of finding dead bodies, either."

Juho stopped to contemplate Sanna's last words. Then he stood up, took Sanna's face between his hands and gave her a long kiss.

"My intention is to be present in body and soul always with you."

"Thank you for understanding what I meant. Apropos, did you tell your sister about me?"

"I didn't have time to say anything; Marjukka knows well enough when her kid brother is in love. She hasn't given up hope of me finding a really good-sensed wifey," Juho replied.

"If she's anything like you, I would love to meet her," Sanna's speech was interrupted by a wide yawn.

"I'm sorry! I didn't sleep very well last night for some reason."

"I should have grasped how tough a weekend you had."

They stood up from the table and Juho showed Sanna the way to the bedroom. Sanna stalled beside the bed, surprised as she saw an open suitcase on top of it with her clothes and other overnight things inside of it.

"Have you been ransacking my closets?" Sanna wondered.

"As a matter of fact, Anu brought them here last night. We agreed on this in the hospital."

"What did Anu say to you in order to convince you to take me in?" Sanna demanded, a little piqued.

"Anu said nothing of the sort. We were both worried about you coping. You should ask for help occasionally. We all want to contribute when you have a rough patch."

Sanna sighed with pleasure. She asked Juho to help her get out of her jeans and jumper before burrowing under the duvet.

"What are you going to do now? Are you coming in as well? Do I really have to sleep alone?" Sanna asked sleepily.

"It is better if you sleep now in peace. It will do you the world of good."

"And I thought I could get my sleeping buddy to join me in here."

"Maybe later. Now you have to be satisfied with a kiss and a hug."

"Lucky me, having something to dream of."

Juho bent down to hug Sanna, giving her the promised kiss. He was tempted to stay but she needed her peaceful rest and nothing else. He sat for a moment beside Sanna on the side of the bed, holding her hand. Making sure she was deep in her sleep, he left the room quietly and went to the living room to do some of his own chores.

Sanna woke up after a couple of hours, hearing noises coming from the living room. It took her a few minutes to catch up as to her whereabouts. She let her sentiments spin around her head without wanting to rise, but the sensation on her lower abdomen made her understand the need to pee. In the living room, she saw Juho sitting on the sofa, his laptop on his knees. At the sight of Sanna, he waved his hand and signalled her nearer, but she pointed to the bathroom, crossing her legs and looking agonised. He thumbed as a sign of understanding, before continuing his conversation. On Sanna's return, he said: "Come here! I want to introduce you to somebody."

As Sanna did what she was told, she saw a young boy on the laptop screen.

"Samuli, this is Sanna. Sanna, this is Samuli."

The boy took a look at Sanna's battered face for a while, before asking: "Were you involved in the same fight with my dad?"

"In a way, yes. One bloke practiced parkour jumps in my flat. When your dad tried to intervene, I hit him with a door by accident."

"I gather you are not one of my dad's workmates."

"I'm afraid I'm not. I am a pharmacist. I suppose there

is no way I could ever do the police stuff, anyway. It was nice meeting you. I think I'll lay down for a while more."

Sanna rose from the sofa and strode towards the bedroom. However, she didn't go back to bed but rather began to go over the contents of the suitcase. Anu had obviously managed to pack everything she needed for a few days' visit. Once she had finished with her inventory, she sat on the bed, contemplating having a shower. She asked Juho for a towel when he had finished his call. He helped Sanna to undress and then they wrapped Sanna's splint into a watertight pack, using a plastic bag and painter's tape.

After the shower, Juho carried Sanna back to the bedroom, both only wearing towels wrapped around them. On the bed, they began wiping each other dry, caressing and kissing each other heatedly.

"I have been bothered by one thing for a long time now," Juho began.

"Only one thing? Is it something I can help you with?" Sanna enquired.

"I've been wondering how Anu recognised me before I had a chance to say anything. All she said was that Jaana had portrayed me, after seeing me only once," Juho was amazed.

"Oh, that thing! In her eyes, you are an actual stunner. The ultimate wet daydream of all the doctors' wives, thanks to which there was a lot of marital sex going on in many beds that night."

Sanna chuckled.

"How's that different from extramarital sex? I have no experience of that."

"Marital sex is the kind when just a gaze or touch can be the foreplay they need. Sometimes, you need a primer to set the flare properly," Sanna went on, still giggling.

"And it was me operating as the primer that night?"

"I suppose so. Everybody was putting their best foot forward and boozing their heads off. You were the cherry on the top."

"Well, I thought I knew everything at this age. I must pay attention to it at the next banquet."

He had the same rush of laughter as Sanna had, imagining the after-party.

"I would be quite happy having some extramarital sex. Just saying," Sanna caressed him.

This time, they had no need to ponder whether somebody would come to interrupt them. Therefore, they were able to surrender to each other at length. After making love, they stayed lying on the bed, holding each other tightly, half asleep. Sanna's last sentiment before falling asleep was: now is good.